Fuhrer's Heart

Fuhrer's Heart

An American Story

James D. Ward

Copyright © 2024 by James D. Ward.

| ISBN: | Softcover | 979-8-3694-2858-0 |
| | eBook | 979-8-3694-2857-3 |

All rights reserved. No part of this book may be reproduced or transmitted in any form or by any means, electronic or mechanical, including photocopying, recording, or by any information storage and retrieval system, without permission in writing from the copyright owner.

This is a work of fiction. Names, characters, places and incidents either are the product of the author's imagination or are used fictitiously, and any resemblance to any actual persons, living or dead, events, or locales is entirely coincidental.

Any people depicted in stock imagery provided by Getty Images are models, and such images are being used for illustrative purposes only.
Certain stock imagery © Getty Images.

Print information available on the last page.

Rev. date: 10/22/2024

To order additional copies of this book, contact:
Xlibris
844-714-8691
www.Xlibris.com
Orders@Xlibris.com
850681

Chapter One

Michael had come a long way since picking cotton and the hot summers down South. Although he was now in the middle of studying for his public law exam and overdosed on case law; he could not help thinking of those days. The thought of small hands picking fluffy white textures of cotton was a bit of a respite. He'd take the cotton from its thorny brown bows and place it gently in the long-textured sack strapped to his mother's shoulder. He could picture his mother, standing beside him, doing the same. Suddenly, he was thrust back into present day reality.

"Oh, no!"

"Is there a problem?" he asked the young woman standing beside the library stacks, next to the table where he was studying, after she had made the sudden nose.

"I was reaching for this code book but I pulled several of them out at once. I am sorry if I bothered you."

"Don't worry about it," said Michael. He grabbed the books from the library floor and handed them to her. "Are you a first-year law student?"

"I'm a third year," she responded. "But, if you need it, I work with a group that helps first year students get established. The first year is the toughest. Believe me."

"I believe you," responded Michael, smiling. "But, I'm not in law school. I'm a graduate student in public policy. I started my doctoral work last semester. I already have my masters."

"Oh," she said, in a pleasant surprise. "That's good to know. My name is Jane, by the way. Pleased to meet you."

"I'm Michael. And I'm pleased to meet you too."

Michael paused and then remarked, "If you're like me, you're going to be hungry in a couple of hours. So, why don't we meet in the student center, get something to eat, and talk some more."

"I believe the student center is a safe place to meet you," replied Jane. So sure, I'll see you there."

"Good," said Michael. "I'll see you at 12:30." Jane smiled and nodded in agreement.

Michael was attracted to Jane at the instant he saw her. He assumed she was attracted to him as well, or at least curious enough to meet him for lunch.

He hoped she would indeed show up. It was 12:45 and she had not arrived. He would wait fifteen more minutes and then leave.

"I'm surprised you are still here but I am glad you waited," Jane said cheerfully as she approached the table.

"I'm glad you came," responded Michael. "What are we eating?"

"I usually get something light, like tacos and a salad."

"Tacos it is," replied Michael, as they approached the counter.

She picked up the mild sauce and Michael opted for the hot and spicy. "Doesn't that burn your mouth?" Jane asked.

"No, I like it spicy."

After two months the friendship blossomed into a romantic relationship. It was a time when they both needed someone special in their lives. They had worked hard in their studies. Now, they realized how important it was to have someone who cared about the little things that go wrong in one's day as well as the triumphs.

In so many ways they were right for each other. Both ambitious, young, African American, and with an unyielding belief in themselves. They made a handsome couple. Jane was a Chicago native. Both her parents were attorneys. The fact that Michael's background was so different made her admire him all the more.

It has been said that the best measure of success is to see how far one has come rather than where one is. That is how Jane saw Michael. She realized that his background was the source of his strength.

While Michael was home, relaxing in the recliner near the window and watching the television news, one of his two female housemates entered the living room. "Well, it's unusual to see you around here at dinner time," said the short and stocky Judy, as she seated herself on the sofa, and as her dirty blonde hair rested at shoulders length. "I know your work and class schedules haven't changed. So, what's keeping you out of the house, stranger?"

"If you must know, I've met someone," Michael replied.

"Oh! Does Rosalind know?" Judy asked.

"No one knows. I like it that way."

"So, when do we get to meet this mystery woman? Or, do we?"

"You will. Maybe I'll invite her over for dinner one night. Or, maybe we can all go out to lunch one Sunday after church."

"I prefer dinner," quickly replied Judy.

"That's fine," said Michael, realizing Judy's lack of affinity for anything religious.

"I'll see if she can come over for dinner Friday night."

"I'll look forward to it," replied Judy, as she began to relax on the sofa.

Michael glanced over at Judy and grinned. He then turned his attention back to the news, adjusting the recliner farther back.

Later that evening, when Michael was in his bedroom reading, Judy telephoned Rosalind at the library, where she worked.

"I've got news for you girl."

"What?" replied the plumb, brown skinned woman.

"I don't want you to be disappointed. But Michael has met someone. Apparently, that's why we haven't seen him much lately."

"Well. He's been quite clear that I'm not his type. What's she like?"

"I don't know," answered Judy. "I guess we'll find out Friday when she comes over for dinner."

"She's coming to the house for dinner?"

"He's gonna see if she can make it. I can't wait."

"Me either."

Michael woke up the next morning, showered and prepared for class. He went into the kitchen for a quick breakfast where he found Rosalind and Judy talking.

"Jane said she'll have dinner with us on Friday," Michael said to Judy.

"Great," replied Judy, as she took a final swallow of orange juice before loading books into her backpack. "Will it be okay if I invite Nick and Jamie?"

"Sure, that's fine," responded Michael. "Even though they're hippies it'll keep me from being the only guy here."

"You live with a hippie," quickly replied Judy. "Always remember that."

"How can we forget it," smirked Rosalind.

"Very smart," Judy smirked back, looking at her watch. "I gotta class. I gotta go."

"Wait for me," touted Rosalind, grabbing her books from the chair next to where she was seated. "I need to ride with you."

Michael soon realized that one of the advantages of knowing Jane was her thorough knowledge of Chicago politics. She and Michael, along with Judy, Rosalind, and other friends, would spend hours playing armchair quarterback for Mayor Harold Washington and arguing over how his administration could best hold at bay the remnants of the feisty Chicago machine led by Bruce Malkovich.

The group gathered one evening in April 1984 in honor of Jane's upcoming graduation. "We are going to miss you so much but we're so proud of you," said one of her female law school friends.

"As you already know," Michael announced, Jane has accepted a job with a black-owned south side law firm, known for its civil rights litigation. I'm so proud of her."

"We're all proud of her," the group responded, almost in unison.

Michael had three years of graduate school to complete when Jane embarked on her law career. Altogether, he spent six years at the University of Chicago. In his final year, while he was writing his dissertation, his major professor, Jack Smith, suggested that he put together a research paper proposal and submit it to the National Association for Political Research (NAPR).

Michael was thrilled when the acceptance letter came in the mail. For the first time his research findings would be presented at a professional conference to scholars considered experts in the field of public policy. Michael's paper was entitled, "A Time-Series Analysis of Privatized Service Delivery in Urban America: Comparing Costs and Benefits."

NAPR had held its annual meeting in Chicago since 1898. This was a gathering of some of the nation's most distinguished social scientists. Among them was Professor Stan Tullock, whose most recent book, *The New Racism: Insights into Modern Conservatism*, was receiving critical acclaim in liberal academic circles.

After the ceremony where the association gave Tullock its prize for the best new book, Jack Smith, a longtime associate of Tullock's, called Michael to a corner of the banquet hall.

"This is Michael Woods. He's one of our most promising PhD candidates."

"I saw your name on the program," said Tullock to Michael. "Interesting paper you wrote."

"You read it?"

"Yes. Jack sent me a copy. You do good work. I'd like to talk to my staff at Orleans about inviting you down for an interview. We're recruiting in your subfield. Would you be interested?"

"I'd be honored," replied Michael. "I'll get a copy of my vitae to you."

"Good. Do that," said Tullock.

Before he had a chance to shake Michael's hand, another eager listener had his attention.

"Excellent networking, Michael," said Jack Smith, touching Michael's shoulder. Michael sensed that Jack was proud to be his mentor. "Tullock is impressed with you. You've done well."

But a possible interview would simply be one in a long list of possibilities. Black PhDs were in high demand and could chart their own paths. Michael had already interviewed at Princeton, Michigan, and USC.

"How well they treat you in the interview is an indication of how well they will treat you once you are there," Jack had advised him months earlier during an office visit, as Michael prepared for his very first job interview. And, the professor's words rung in Michael's ears upon his arrival at Moisant International Airport. Orleans was the first university that had sent a limousine to take him to his hotel. Even Princeton hadn't tried so hard to impress him.

The university, referred to simply as "Orleans," had been founded in 1739 by Bertrand Thibodeaux, governor of Louisiana before the territory belonged to the United States. Steeped in French Creole tradition, it had resisted delivering lectures in the English language until 1868, more than 60 years after the Louisiana Purchase.

During Michael's visit he was subjected to brief individual interview sessions with each faculty member in the university's Institute for Public Policy. This took two and a half days. The 30-minute sessions did little to provide Michael with a grasp of the personalities that made up the Institute. The arrangement did, however, allow the Institute's faculty to size up Michael.

On the final day of the interview, several professors gave Michael a tour of the campus, which stretched from the Garden District to the river. Michael had never seen such majestic mansions.

"Apparently there is a lot of money at Orleans," he said. "How heavily endowed is the university?"

"I'm not sure," answered Elliott Nussmeyer. "But I believe the latest report put it at close to nine hundred million dollars."

"Well, it's almost time for you to meet one on one with our director," said Doris Neuhaus, looking at her watch. "We'd better be heading back."

"How long has Dr. Schultz been director?" asked Michael.

"Only a year," replied Henry Murphy. "Directors and academic department heads are appointed and reviewed every three years. She has two more years left."

Doris Neuhaus and Elliott Nussmeyer were silent.

"So, you've survived your second full day," said Dr. Mitzie Schultz as Michael walked into her office with his three guides.

"It wasn't that bad," responded Michael.

"Well, we'll leave you two alone," said Nussmeyer. "It was good meeting you Dr. Woods."

"Nice meeting all of you too," responded Michael, as he shook each of their hands.

"Have a seat," said Mitzie as she closed the door and seated herself behind her desk. Michael was amazed at the generous salary and teaching load she offered and at how businesslike she was in cutting to the chase. Michael smiled. He never dreamed he could come out of graduate school making such a hefty salary. He now had no regrets about saying no to law school.

"Did you enjoy the limousine?"

"Yes. I did. Thank you."

"Well, just our way of letting you know you're important to us. However, we also want you to get familiar as possible with a cross section of our graduate students. So, Nikki Kraus will drive you back to the airport this afternoon. She's one of our MA's."

"That's her now," said Dr. Schultz, as she got up to answer the door. "Nikki, you've met our candidate Dr. Woods?"

"I was at your research presentation this morning," responded Nikki, as she shook Michael's hand. "I enjoyed it."

As Michael and Nikki walked out of the building and toward Nikki's car, Michael could not help but notice how much Nikki reminded him of the white sorority girls back at UVA. She was polished and definitely from a southern family with money.

"I saw on your vitae that you graduated from UVA in '81," said Nikki, as they drove off to the airport. "I know someone who was there at that time. His name's Jim DeLashmet. Did you know him?"

"Not personally," replied Michael, "although our paths did cross once or twice. I worked on the school paper. He was president of campus senate, I think."

"Yes, that's him," responded Nikki. "He's from my high school. He's a lawyer here in town now. Maybe you should give him a phone call once you move down."

Michael was taken off guard by the graduate student's comment. Did she know something he did not?

"You mean if I get the job, don't you?" he responded.

"Oh, you'll get it," said Nikki.

"Do you have a favorite professor at the Institute?" asked Michael.

"Well, I'd have to say Matt Kohl. I've been his research assistant since I started the MA program. We think a lot alike."

"I didn't meet him. Did I?"

"No. He's been in Austria since January. He's visiting professor at the University of Innsbruck. He'll be back at the end of the summer."

"Oh, I see," remarked Michael. "That's impressive."

Once on the airplane Michael could relax and think over the events of the last three days. On the whole he felt extremely positive. He had enjoyed his meeting with graduate students and thought his interviews with the faculty had gone well. If offered the job, he decided he would take it.

The faculty met almost immediately after Michael's departure. The meeting was rushed because they knew Michael already had one job offer and possibly others forthcoming.

"He seems like a pleasant sort," remarked Professor Barry Bonds. "I think he would fit in pretty well."

"What about Maggie Abramson? I liked her, even if she is from New York," said John Walker. "Doesn't that count for something?"

"It would," explained Stan Tullock, "except we already have two women. We don't need to hire another white woman."

"He seems nice enough," onerously claimed Barney Holtz. "He might even get tenure."

Mitzie Schultz smiled and silently nodded. Most of the other faculty members did the same. "Okay. Let's vote by a show of hands on whether to hire Michael Woods," said Mitzie. "Only if the vote is negative will we vote on the other candidates. Those in favor? Those opposed? Okay.

The vote was fourteen to five in favor. Michael Woods will be offered the job."

"That's it!" shouted John Walker as he marched out of the room in protest and slammed the door behind him. Henry Murphy and Orville Reid, two other faculty members who had voted with Walker and against Michael, gritted their teeth and followed Walker out of the room. The remaining two, Harry Bernstein and Alex Sanchez, turned their faces toward the wall and stared at it to express their disagreement.

"Well, you can't please all the people all the time," said Mitzie. "This meeting has served its purpose and it is adjourned."

The next day she called Michael. He accepted the job.

Michael spent most of the summer planning his move to New Orleans and seeing as much of Jane as time permitted. He wrote letters to his friends from college. He also wrote letters to his graduate school buddies who had since moved away.

At the university, Jack Smith was the most proud of Michael's achievement. It reflected well on him and on the department, and he took every opportunity to mention it during department meetings and even college and university-wide functions.

Michael arrived in New Orleans the last week in July. He found his new colleagues eager to help him adjust to Louisiana. But he soon realized that it would take him months even to begin to understand the personalities that defined the Institute's power center.

Mitzie Schultz, being the director, would have the most influence on his success. She was a petite blue-eyed blonde who had somehow preserved for herself an aura of upper middle-class privilege. She had short hair and she was always neatly dressed like a 1960s boarding school product.

From Michael's perspective, Barry Bonds appeared more difficult to get to know. During his interview Bonds had seemed outright antagonistic. He had said that Michael's applied research focus would weaken the Institute. Instinctively, Michael sensed that something much deeper troubled Bonds, but he could not put his finger on it. So, he smiled and explained that his research targeted salient public policy issues including the environment, productivity, and equal opportunity.

He had gathered that Bonds was highly statistical, which would explain his lack of interest in qualitative research on policy issues. Nevertheless, Michael was surprised that his smiles and good manners seemed to have won Bonds over.

Michael had met Stan Tullock, Doris Neuhaus, Ralph Lee and Barney Holtz at the conference in Chicago, so having seen them again during his interview was more of a reacquaintance and made it easier for him to feel relaxed with them once he started work.

Michael spent much of his first month in New Orleans preparing his fall classes. During the steamy summer afternoons, he was often alone at the Institute, but one day he saw a light in the office with the name Ralph Lee on the door.

"Hello. I'm teaching policy implementation this fall," said Michael, as he stuck his head into Ralph Lee's office. "I was wondering if I could talk to you about approach, since you last taught the class here."

"Sure," said Ralph, looking up from his desk with an inscrutable expression on his face. "Come on in."

"Perhaps I can review the syllabus you used," Michael suggested.

"No problem," said Ralph in his distinctively southern drawl. "I'll gladly share that information with you."

"Okay," said Michael. "I think the students will appreciate my trying to respect the type of instructional approach they're accustomed to."

"I'm sure they will," agreed Ralph. "You know, I am a genuine southerner. You should know that. I was born and bred in the heart of Dixie. That's Alabama - Decatur. Although I was raised in Cullman. Anyway, I'm proud to be a southerner. It runs in my veins."

Michael's response was guarded. "That's interesting."

"I have three degrees from Ole Miss," added Ralph, a slender fiftyish man whose thinning dark hair was streaked with gray. "I remember the riots when those two outside agitators were shot to death over the admission of James Meredith. I was a graduate student back then when that happened."

Michael's eyes opened wider. More information was coming his way than he was willing to digest.

"Ole Miss!" said Ralph, as his face flushed with kindred emotion. "Her heart, even today, is the soul of the Old South. That's one university where every true southerner, regardless of where in the South he was born, can rest assured that he is home."

"Well, that's good to know," responded Michael, as he sat across from Ralph's desk with his note pad in his hand. "However, I only wanted to get a little input from you on the policy implementation course. Which textbooks did you use?"

"Oh! Yes. Forgive my flashbacks," said Ralph, as his face began to reveal a slight embarrassment. "I sometimes get carried away by nostalgia. But I'm harmless."

"I'm sure you are," said Michael, smiling.

"To answer your question," said Ralph, "I used *Policy Implementation and Organizational Change*. It's the book by Ron Thomas at Harvard. It's probably the best text in the field these days. Oh! Let me get a copy of that syllabus for you."

Ralph got up and opened the second drawer to his filing cabinet. He pulled out a folder labeled Class Syllabi, and thumbed through it. "Here, here it is. You can have this copy. I have others."

"Thank you," said Michael, as he took the syllabus. "It was nice hearing about your past. Maybe we can talk again later."

"Thanks for stopping by," replied Ralph. Michael gave Ralph a friendly wave and left the room.

Ralph was not like most of the other faculty, most of whom were midwesterners with graduate degrees from Big Ten universities. Yet they all prided themselves on being progressive liberals of the new South. They were mostly in their 40s and 50s. Doris, 34, and Michael, 28, were the youngest Institute professors.

Michael soon learned that this liberal group made up the Institute's power center. But soon he met John Walker. Unlike those in the power circle, who were mostly protestant, John Walker was catholic. He was a California native who had done graduate work at Stanford. And he was a political conservative and the black sheep of the Institute

Walker knocked on Michael's office door one late September morning. "I just thought I would stop by and officially introduce myself. I'm John Walker."

"I know," said Michael. "I saw you at the faculty meeting last week."

"Well, how are you getting situated here?"

"I'm settling in just fine. I am excited about being here."

"Are you free for lunch?"

"Yes. I am." Michael was surprised. "Just let me put these books away and we can leave. You wanna go on or off campus?"

"I thought we'd just walk over to the University Club, if that's okay with you."

"That sounds good."

Michael and John Walker had lunch together several times. Michael found that he shared John's conservatism when it came to fiscal matters but differed with John on many social issues such as civil rights and affirmative action.

"I judge you based on your qualifications, not your race like some of my colleagues," John told Michael one day at lunch. "You have impeccable credentials. I'm glad you are here."

"Thanks, I appreciate that."

Michael was surprised to hear John put so much emphasis on race. But John was opposed to affirmative action, so it made sense.

Matt Kohl finally got around to inviting Michael to a get acquainted lunch. It was one month after Michael had first had lunch with John Walker. To say the least, Professor Matt Kohl was not what Michael had hoped he would be. He was a cold and distant man. Michael had realized such weeks earlier when he asked Kohl to review one of his manuscripts before he sent it out for journal review.

"We hired you, but you shouldn't expect any special treatment just because you're a minority," Kohl saw fit to respond.

"I know," agreed Michael. "But President Hodge Williams said assistant professors should solicit advice before sending out manuscripts. He said it would speed up the publication process."

"We don't have time to hold assistant professor's hands," said Kohl.

Kohl had a large physical presence, an intimidating personality and a deep and overbearing voice. The fact that Kohl seemed to wield more than his share of influence at the Institute made him all the more powerful.

Michael spent less and less time thinking about Kohl as the months went by. His time and energy were occupied by his work.

After returning to his office from a morning class Michael received a telephone call from Doris Neuhaus.

"I need to discuss something with you. Can you have dinner with me tonight?"

"Yes, I can."

"Okay, good. What about seven o'clock at Lula Mae's Creole Kitchen? It's on Chartres Street."

"What do you want to talk to me about?"

"I'd rather wait until then," said Doris.

As Michael parked his car on Barracks Street and walked towards Chartres, he noticed a sign that read: "Old New Orleans Slave Exchange." The slave exchange was now a touristy restaurant with fine wines and fine foods served on white linen tablecloths. It was a busy place. Michael was taken with the rich history in New Orleans.

Lula Mae's was a modest little restaurant. Doris was already there, seated at a quaint wooden table. Her long white legs, crossed at the knees, stretched out from beside the table, revealing her low-heeled, casual dress pumps. At five feet seven, Doris had shoulder length blonde hair and green eyes. She was beautiful. She raised her arm at the elbow and slightly wiggled her front two fingers at Michael as he entered Lula Mae's. She then uncrossed her legs and put both knees underneath the table and out of sight.

"The food here is good and the prices aren't bad.," she said as Michael pulled out the chair and sat down. "It's very reasonable for a French Quarter restaurant."

"Hey, that's good to know," replied Michael, as he glanced at the menu. "What is it that you want to talk to me about?"

"It's about the Institute," said Doris, as she was interrupted by the waiter.

"Are you ready to order?" he asked. The waiter was a young black man in his early twenties. This surprised Michael because he rarely saw a black waiter in French Quarter restaurants. An old New Orleans service industry tradition dictated that whites provide table service and that blacks, usually poor and uneducated, be the dishwashers. But Lula Mae's was a black owned restaurant, one of only two in the French Quarter.

"I'm having the crawfish etouffee and iced tea," said Doris.

"And, do you need more time, sir?" asked the waiter.

"No," replied Michael. "I'll have the shrimp jambalaya platter and just a tall glass of water to drink."

"Oh, yes!" said Doris to the waiter. "There is one more person coming so I'm ordering a second crawfish etouffee platter along with an extra glass of water."

"Okay," said the waiter, as he walked away from the table.

"Who else is coming?" asked Michael

"A friend of mine," replied Doris, quickly looking at her watch. "I thought it would be good for you to meet him. He'll be here at 7:15."

"That's good," said Michael. "Is he a professor?"

"He teaches at the community college," replied Doris. Adding, in a more businesslike tone, "Anyway, what I want to tell you is important."

"What is it?"

"Well, you should know that there are certain factions at the Institute and you should therefore be careful where you step."

"Oh really," said Michael, not letting her on to the fact that he had already figured this out."

"Basically, there was a fight over hiring you. John Walker was on the losing side. I'm sure you know the rest. What you don't know is that John Walker has made enemies with some very powerful people here over the years. So, if you want a future here, I suggest you pick your friends more carefully."

Michael was caught off guard by Doris' forceful and bossy attitude. After all, who was she? He did not like the idea of her telling him who his friends could and could not be. But he was too new to start rocking any boats. He would think about what Doris said and avoid John Walker, if need be.

Shortly thereafter, in walked Tyrone Lockett, a young black man who looked about Michael's age.

"Hello," said Doris as she got up and hugged the young black man. "Tyrone, this is Michael, our new faculty member."

"Welcome to the Big Easy," said Tyrone as he took a seat.

"Thanks," replied Michael, surprised that Doris had a black boyfriend. "I'm happy to be here."

"Would you like to go Cajun dancing with us after dinner," Doris asked Michael.

"You have to," said Tyrone. "You're new in town. You gotta get a taste of some local flavor."

"It's a Friday night. So, there is no excuse not to. Right?"

"Right," said Doris.

"Right," said Tyrone.

They first went to Muddy Waters to hear Buckwheat Zydeco and then ended up at the Maple Leaf where the Rock'n Dopsie Band was playing. Michael could easily tell that Doris was a superb dancer and that she had taught Tyrone well. Their Cajun dance looked like a square dance with rhythm. It was perfect for the zydeco music being played.

"What exactly is zydeco?" Michael asked Doris while she and Tyrone took a break from dancing.

"It's a mixture of Cajun and jazz," Doris answered, looking into Michael's eyes. "A blend of Louisiana musical cultures."

"That's interesting," responded Michael, "It's like a marriage."

"Right," agreed Doris, as revelers danced in the background. "Have you been married?"

"No," I haven't," answered Michael, "but I have a girlfriend. She is in Chicago."

"I've been married," Doris said to Michael.

"Any children?" he asked.

"No, can't have children," responded Doris.

"I didn't know that!" interjected Tyrone, having overhead their conversation.

Doris briefly glanced at Tyrone, then turned her attention back to Michael, ignoring Tyrone's comment.

The band started playing Doris' favorite song. Doris took Michael by the hand and attempted to dance with him. "I'm sorry," said Michael. "I don't know how to do it."

When Michael went to get another drink, Tyrone and Doris returned to the dance floor. Eventually, the night petered out slowly, as Michael thanked the couple for a terrific evening and headed back to his car, getting home around three o'clock in the morning. The following week, Tyrone telephoned Michael asked if he'd be interested in a nighttime tennis match. Michael accepted.

They met on the community college campus where Tyrone taught English. "My life's ambition is to be a writer," said Tyrone, as they walked from the parking lot towards the tennis courts. "That's why I'm teaching English here."

"I guess mine is somewhat similar," responded Michael. "But, scholarly writing."

"You're definitely gonna have to do some writing if you stay at the Institute," replied Tyrone.

"That, I know," agreed Michael.

Once the match started, Michael found himself unprepared for Tyrone's ferocious hard serve and volley. Although Michael was an above average player, Tyrone's sharp competitive mood was too much for him.

After Tyrone won the tennis match, the two talked for about an hour in the parking lot. Before long, however, their talk centered solely on Doris.

"I played tennis once or twice a week in Chicago," said Michael. "But it was mostly for the exercise. Hardly ever did I play anyone as competitive as you."

"I could easily have other women," said Tyrone. Had he even heard what Michael had said? "I could have beautiful creole women. But I choose to stay with her."

Michael could see the pain in Tyrone's face as he spoke of Doris. He thought about the previous week outside the Maple Leaf when Doris, in her tight skirt, had danced very suggestively up against him on the sidewalk. Michael remembered Tyrone's strange reaction.

Perhaps, Michael thought, Tyrone's love was not being returned. Maybe he was being used. Michael did not know. However, Michael did hold to the notion that there were some white women out there who were attracted to black men but allowed societal pressure to prevent a meaningful relationship from being established. He wondered how much of this explained Tyrone's problem with Doris.

Even if he was right, Michael had learned not to jump to conclusions. He kept his opinions to himself and chose not to offer any advice.

"You know," he said to Tyrone, "I have this beautiful woman in Chicago that I'm madly in love with. So, just in case it crossed your mind, don't even think about fixing me up with any of these New Orleans ladies."

Tyrone suddenly appeared more relaxed. "So, you're a married man, huh?"

"All except for the paperwork," said Michael.

Several weeks elapsed without Michael doing anything else socially with either Doris or Tyrone. But later in the semester one afternoon in December, Michael looked up and saw Doris tapping on his open office door. She was not her usual cheerful self. "Is something wrong?" he asked.

"Tyrone and I have had a fight."

"A fight?"

"Yes, a fight. I need someone to talk to. You have a minute?"

"Sure. Have a seat."

Doris seated herself in one of the two empty chairs in Michael's office. "I know it's all because he cannot control me," she mused. "He is a very jealous and insecure man."

"I'm sorry to hear that," said Michael.

"He's been that way since I met him but it got worse early in the semester, around the time we went dancing. He was angry and short tempered every time I saw him after that."

"Maybe his insecurity lies in the fact that he loves you so much and he's afraid that he may lose you."

Doris looked up at the ceiling and opened her palms as if searching for an answer. "Why on the earth does he need to control me?" She then placed her hands over her face. "Last night," she said, placing her hands back down on her lap, "we got into an argument and he started yelling so loud and swinging his fists. I thought he was going to hit me. I was so afraid."

"Wow," said Michael. He searched for the proper response, but he didn't know what to say.

"I just needed someone to talk to," quietly replied Doris, tears filling her eyes. "He called me a slut."

"My God!" said Michael.

Michael saw a vulnerable woman who needed comfort but he knew he was not the person to give it. At this moment he did not trust his feelings.

"I'd love to talk to you about this, but I have all this work to do," Michael said, as he opened a book on his desk.

"I understand," said Doris, as she stood up and began to walk to the door. "You've been a big help. Thanks."

"Oh! No trouble. I hope everything works out for you."

Michael was glad Doris was gone. He did not trust himself in vulnerable situations with her. And, to make matters even more interesting, by the end of the week, Doris and Tyrone were back together.

Michael again remembered Tyrone's reaction when he overheard Doris telling him things at the Maple Leaf. Perhaps, Michael thought, Tyrone knew in his heart that Doris would never give herself totally to him. That would explain Tyrone's rage.

By the beginning of the spring semester, it was obvious to Michael that Doris preferred black men. In addition, she was by far the most liberal of the liberals at the Institute. She often referred to herself as a leftist. Michael first heard Doris described herself that way during her January colloquium. She had presented her research on right-wing hate groups and American political ideology.

Michael realized that of the fifteen professors present only he seemed surprised when Doris said "we leftists." He assumed the other professors were used to it.

It seemed especially odd for Doris to call herself a leftist, because she was on the mailing list of several white supremacist groups. Michael had seen the materials in her office mailbox and on her desk.

One February evening following his Wednesday night seminar, he noticed Doris taping some clippings about David Duke and his neo-Nazi rallies to her office door. He stopped by her door.

"You know, I've been meaning to ask you why you subscribe to white supremacist newsletters and place the clippings on your door. Isn't this all kind of odd for a leftist?"

"It helps me keep abreast of their activities," explained Doris. "It's a daily reminder of what's out there. This way I see it every day when I come in to work."

"Yes. And so do the rest of us," remarked Michael.

"That's true," agreed Doris as she picked up some books from her desk and shelved them. "I get David Duke's National Association for the Advancement of White People newsletter. I have copies of Donald Sykes' old White America newsletter, and I have others as well."

"Come to think of it, I had a professor at the University of Chicago who subscribed to communist newsletters and he was not a communist. But I've heard that several professors here invited David Duke and Donald Sykes to speak in their classes. Is that true?

"It's all academic," Doris explained as she seated herself in her swivel chair. "I've done it. So have Barney Holtz and Elliott Nussmeyer. Others have too. It's all because the best way to prevent the spread of this racist garbage is to expose it for what it is."

"And how do you do that?" inquired Michael, still standing inside Doris' door.

"By letting the sun shine on it," answered Doris. "Let's face it. Sunshine disinfects. So does the truth. Disinfectant is at work in the classroom because the racist ideology is being rationally challenged."

"I can understand that," replied Michael.

"I thought you would," said Doris, smiling.

Chapter Two

Somehow Doris Neuhaus managed to transcend the Institute factionalism she had warned Michael about. Although she was indisputably a member of the liberal cohort that ran the Institute, she was also well spoken of by John Walker and his minority faction. Perhaps this was why Harry Bernstein, the transplanted New Yorker, felt comfortable confiding in Doris.

Michael was not quite sure what was going on between them, but he suspected that a friendship, or at least very cordial acquaintance, did exist between Bernstein and Doris. Michael's office was directly across the hallway from Bernstein's. He could hear their conversations. Doris would sometimes be in Bernstein's office two or three times a week. Michael guessed that Bernstein, being Jewish, was impressed with Doris' monitoring of neo-Nazi groups.

Bernstein also frequently talked to John Walker, and Michael could overhear their conversations too. Those conversations made clear to Michael that Bernstein was having serious trouble at the Institute.

Late one February morning, right before lunch, Michael returned to his office from class and saw that Bernstein's door was cracked open. He heard John Walker's voice. Walker and Bernstein were talking louder than usual.

Sitting at his desk, Michael could still hear Bernstein say, "They know I have a book coming out next year. They should give me the final year on my contract so the book can count towards tenure."

"It's not going to happen," Walker told Bernstein. "You know it and I know it. It's not going to happen because of politics. And with you, it's the worst kind of politics. It's personal politics. They don't like you."

Several seconds of silence elapsed. "They don't like me either, for that matter," added John Walker.

Michael got up from his desk and walked out into the hall. He pretended to be taping a class list to the bulletin board next to his door.

"That's beside the point," Bernstein said to John. "You're already tenured."

"You're right," replied John.

"This shit is not fair!" exclaimed Bernstein. "These S-O-B's are going to pay! You wait and see. I'm going to rip these bastards by the balls! Dammit! You have to be Protestant, white, and from the Midwest to succeed at this fucking place."

"Well, I'm going to lunch. You still want to join me?" John asked.

"No," replied Bernstein. "I'm too fucking mad to eat."

Michael quickly walked back into his office, closed his door, and seated himself at his desk.

Michael remembered what John Walker had said to him over lunch last fall. "The Institute was a totally different place 20 years ago when I got this job. That's when Henry Warner, a Jew, was director. Warner made the Institute what it is today, reputation wise. Unfortunately, he retired ten years ago. The place hasn't been the same since."

"What do you mean?"

"What I mean is, it was under Warner's leadership that the Institute gained its international reputation. After his retirement, the current power structure took shape with a vengeance. But when Henry left, there was no longer the overshadowing and admired leader to quench burning fires. Warner was a true leader. Basically, he recruited and cultivated most of the talent that's here now."

Lying in bed that night, Michael thought about the conversation between Bernstein and Walker. If Henry Warner was Jewish, Bernstein must be wrong in assuming the Institute is anti-Semitic. Michael decided he would talk to Doris Neuhaus and Matt Kohl about what he had heard. The next morning, he saw Doris walking across campus. He ran up to her and told her what he had heard.

"I wish I could do something to help Harry," said Doris. "But I can't. Besides you, I have the least seniority here."

"Do you believe the Institute is anti-Semitic?"

"No, I don't!" insisted Doris. "Henry Warner is Jewish. Everyone here loved him. Harry made bad decisions when he mapped out his research strategy several years ago. It just didn't pan out the way he thought it would."

"I kind of figured as much," said Michael.

On the way to his office Michael knocked on Matt Kohl's office door. "Do you have a minute?"

"Yes. What can I do for you?" responded Kohl as he looked up from his computer screen.

"I just have a minor question about expectations for tenure. I want to know how various senior faculty might weigh items differently."

"I'm listening," responded Kohl.

"I happened to overhear Bernstein complaining that although he has a book coming out next year the Institute won't consider it in his evaluation. Why is that?"

"Bernstein doesn't have a book," Kohl strongly asserted. "He has a book contract. He claims it will be published next year but there is no guarantee. The bottom line is that Bernstein is history no matter what he does from here on out. Giving him another year would only prolong the inevitable. That's the consensus."

Michael felt sorry for Bernstein and fearful for his own future at the Institute. Even if Bernstein had failed to meet the standards required for promotion and tenure, it was also clear that Kohl did not like Bernstein. Bernstein seemed to be up a creek without a paddle.

One afternoon in March, exactly six months after Michael had started work at the Institute, an angry Bernstein came over to Michael's office, asked to sit down, and proceeded to inform Michael at length of the injustices that had been perpetrated against him.

"You've probably heard the lies floating around this place about me."

"I'm not sure," responded Michael. "I did hear that they're not giving you the last year of your contract."

"They're out to get rid of me!" Bernstein insisted. "But I am fighting it and I need all the help I can get."

"What kind of help?"

"I need you to keep your eyes open. Keep your ears open," answered Bernstein. "Keep them open for anything you see or hear. Anything that'll show that the decision against me is personal and contrived."

"You have any proof?" asked Michael.

Bernstein paused, looked at Michael, and answered, "You know, they are never going to tenure a black at this place. They're just using you to buy time. You know that, don't you?"

"Why do you say that?" demanded Michael.

Slowly, Bernstein responded, "Because I did everything they told me to do. I got the book deal. I published articles in refereed journals. But, it didn't matter. It never mattered."

"Matt Kohl said you don't have a book," replied Michael. "He says you only have a book contract. He said the faculty had to decide because it was time to finalize the decision regarding your tenure."

"So, he has been talking to you about me!" exclaimed Bernstein. "So, did he tell you that now it doesn't matter what I do from here on out. Is that what he told you?"

"Yes. That's what he said," Michael answered.

"But it should matter!" Bernstein insisted. "It would matter any place else!" He composed himself and continued. "What you must understand is that they knew from the day they hired me how they were going to rule on my promotion and tenure."

Bernstein was already losing the little composure he had. "It's that short, weasel, bastard Barney Holtz who contrived the lie that I had sex with students in my office! The rest of them are just going along with it!" Tears filled Bernstein's eyes. His anger was now mixed with despair, and he grew quiet as he stared into space. Then his emotions reloaded. "These bastards are threatening to bring students in to substantiate these damn lies if I don't leave quietly! Either way, my career is ruined!"

Bernstein began to sweat profusely. "You see how important it is that you help me. You are not one of them! You have to do what's right! You have to help me put a stop to this! I'm filing a lawsuit. But I am going to need help from as many people here as I can get! Please help me! Please help us both! Tell the court what Kohl told you."

Michael did not know what to do. "I'm sorry," he said to Bernstein. "I have to go and teach. I wish you well." Michael left Bernstein alone in his office.

The next day, Mitzie stopped Michael in the hall. "We heard what happened," she said. "You know, you were one of the top minority PhDs in the country when we hired you. You should disregard the allegations of a chronic liar like Bernstein."

"Bernstein is being denied tenure," added Matt Kohl, who was standing next to Mitzie, "based on his inability to publish at the level required by a world-renowned Institute."

Michael had not told anyone about Bernstein's visit to his office. Had someone walked by his office while Bernstein was talking to him? Or had Bernstein confided in the wrong person? What was going on? Could things get any worse for Bernstein?

Although Mitzie was Institute director, Michael sensed that Matt Kohl was the king maker, the true power behind the scene. He was an authoritarian who could sometimes be dangerously quiet and observant.

Michael thought Barney Holtz seemed to hate Bernstein even more than Kohl did. Holtz used profanity whenever someone mentioned Bernstein's name in his presence. On the other hand, Holtz often used profanity. He was a short, squat man, completely lacking in charm. Michael wondered how someone like Holtz had ever become a power player. If there were ever such a thing as a blue-collar professor, Holtz was it. He was often seen sitting in his office and eating sardines from the can. Afterward he would lick his fingers clean.

Michael decided to attend to his own business. When Bonds, who also had no affinity for Bernstein, approached Michael about coauthoring a paper for the upcoming NAPR conference, Michael accepted. He knew working with one of the Institute's power players would benefit him.

One afternoon, Holtz ran into Michael in the Institute lounge where Michael was sitting on the rich, leather sofa and reading the latest NAPR newsletter. "A group of people are meeting at The Gator Grill around six o'clock. Why don't you join us?" Holtz said.

"I'll be there," responded Michael. "Thanks."

Michael knew a certain amount of socializing was a part of the job. Yet, he was sure the invitation would prove to be just another attempt on the part of the faculty to lobby him against Bernstein.

Once at Gator's, Michael was surprised to find two students at the table with Holtz and Bonds. One of the students was an undergraduate. Holtz introduced her as Marcia and said that both her parents were professors in the business school. Michael remembered her from last fall. She had intentionally bumped up against him in the hallway while wearing a "Sykes for U.S. Senate" button, as if to say, "you'd better move because I don't have to."

Now, he asked her bluntly, "Why are you a Donald Sykes fan?"

"I wasn't until I took Barney's class," she said. "He told me to write a research paper on Sykes. I did. And I've been a fan ever since."

"It just goes to show, sometimes exposure to the truth does not bring about the desired outcome," chuckled Barney Holtz.

Marcia, sitting beside Holtz, looked up at him and grinned. She was short like Holtz and she had short hair.

"How old are you?" Michael asked.

"I'm 20," said Marcia.

"This is David Piston," said Barry Bonds, glancing at the young man sitting beside him and across from Michael. "He's a graduate student."

"Hello," said Michael.

Piston nodded at Michael but did not say a word to him. He was cold and distant, would not talk, but seemed to be staring at Michael. Just as Michael was thinking about how odd David Piston appeared to be, Doris Neuhaus walked into Gator's and hurriedly came over to where the group was sitting.

"I'm surprised to see you here," David said to her. This was the first time Michael had heard David's voice.

"Yes, but I'm not staying very long," replied Doris, as she grabbed a chair and pulled it up to the table between Michael and Marcia. "I have more work to do in the office tonight."

"That's where I'll be too," said Michael. "I've got that conference this week."

"Yeah, me too," said Doris.

"May I get you something to drink ma'am?" asked the young student waitress.

"Just coffee," answered Doris.

"How would you like that ma'am? Cream and sugar?"

"No. Black."

"What ever happened to Nikki Kraus?" Michael asked the group. "She was the graduate student who took me to the airport after my interview. Is she still around? I haven't seen her."

The table was silent. "She transferred to Tufts right before the start of the fall semester," Holtz finally answered. "She didn't like it here."

"That's odd," said Michael. "When I talked to her, she seemed so happy. What didn't she like?"

Again, there was silence. The silence was deafening. Finally, Barney Holtz spoke.

"She didn't say."

"I think she's happy back in the Northeast where she went to undergraduate school," added Doris.

"Her family is from here though, right?" asked Michael.

"Right," remarked Doris. "Audubon Place."

"She was okay," said Holtz. "By the way, how is that paper coming along that you and Barry are working on?"

"It's coming along good," Michael replied.

"Just needs a few finishing touches," interjected Bonds. "We'll finish it up tonight."

"Speaking of finishing touches, I think I should get back to it," said Michael. "Perhaps I'll see some of you in Chicago."

"You'll see me in about 30 minutes," responded Bonds.

"Okay. I enjoyed it. Thanks for inviting me, Barney."

"Thank you for coming," replied Holtz.

Michael was responsible for the paper's conceptualization and he did most of the actual writing. Bonds applied multivariate analysis to measure its hypothesis which centered on the relationship between public policy outcomes and the percentage of black elected officials in the South. Bonds stopped by Michael's office shortly afterwards. They worked for a couple of hours, until Bonds said, "Well, it's ten o'clock so I'm out of here."

"I'm going to stay a little longer," said Michael.

"Okay," replied Bonds. He walked down to Doris' office. They briefly chatted. Michael could tell when they both left the building because it became quiet.

Michael often worked on his research projects until late at night. Tonight, when he glanced at his watch, he saw that it was two o'clock in the morning. He had been at his computer for five hours straight. He had been working hard. But he knew that hard work would pay off. This was the way it had always been for Michael, especially in college and graduate school.

After a good night's sleep, Michael returned to the office at nine o'clock. "Good morning, Dr. Woods," said Gracie Mullen, the head secretary, as he walked into the main office to check his mailbox. "We made copies of your conference paper for you. They're there in your mailbox."

"Thanks, Gracie," responded Michael, as he retrieved his mail and copies of his paper, "Thanks so much."

"No problem," said Gracie.

Michel walked down the hallway with joyful anticipation. He would be in Chicago in eight hours. Entering his office, he opened his attaché case and looked inside. He wanted to make sure he had everything he needed for the conference. He counted the number of copies of the conference paper. NAPR required twenty. While he was checking his airline tickets, John Walker entered his office and said, "Long time, no see."

"I have really been busy," responded Michael.

"Sure, conference and all," replied John.

Michael hesitated and then said, "You know John, to be honest, I have been warned to keep away from you."

"I kinda figured they'd gotten to you," John replied. "However, let me tell you something. I opposed your hiring because of the way they were doing it. I had nothing against you then and I have nothing against you now."

"Thank you," responded Michael.

John turned to leave the room. He stopped, turned back around and said, "I believe you should know that the only other black hired by this Institute was hired nine years ago. He was hired because of his race and fired because of it. You're too good for that." John briskly left the room and went back to his own office down the hall.

Michael did not know whether John's remarks were just another expression of Institute factionalism and hatred for liberal policies or whether they were true. After several moments of thought Michael brushed John's comments aside. After all, thinking it over, he decided to ignore them. Michael learned long ago that he was different from most other blacks, more adaptable. He was sure that whatever had happened to the other black professor would not happen to him.

After teaching his afternoon class, Michael drove straight to the airport. He could hardly wait to see Jane again. She had visited him twice in New Orleans. It had been three months since he had seen her. Soon he would be able to caress her beautiful brown skin and touch her shoulder length hair. She was waiting at the gate, smiling. He embraced her with one arm, holding his garment bag and attaché case with the other. She put her arm around his waist.

"How was your flight?" she asked.

"I spent the whole time thinking about you."

"Right answer," she responded. Adding, "I often wonder what your life is like without me down there in New Orleans."

"It's almost empty," answered Michael.

Jane smiled, looked up at Michael, and said, "Your answers are getting better and better." They then briefly caressed on the way to Jane's car.

After arriving downtown, Michael checked into the Grand Plaza Hotel, where the lobby was filled with public policy professors from around the country. It was the beginning of a warm reunion. Jane still lived at home with her parents. So, she decided to take Michael up on his offer to spend the night at the hotel with him.

"It's so good to be with you," said Michael, as they lay in bed. "I wish you would move to New Orleans." Michael paused, thought for a few seconds, and then said, "Of course, I would never ask you to do such a thing before first making you my wife."

"What!" Jane laughingly responded. "First, allow me time to perform an exploratory investigation into how such an action will impact the dynamics of me."

"Will you marry me, Jane?" asked Michael. "I do love you."

"I love you too Michael," responded Jane in a more serious voice. "You know, I want to spend the rest of my life with you. So, you should not be surprised that my answer is yes."

"Thank you," said Michael, as he gently brushed his finger across Jane's lips. "As I look into your eyes," Michael added, "my heart overflows with love for you. Yet, I want my love for you to honor God. That's the only way I know to go into a marriage."

"I feel the same way," said Jane. "You know that for me, marriage is a one-time deal. I don't believe in divorce. So, it's scary to even think of getting married without doing it God's way."

Michael pressed his lips against hers and gently kissed her. In his heart and soul, Michael thanked God for this beautiful woman. A streak of light came through the slightly parted curtains and lit her face.

The next morning at breakfast in the hotel restaurant they discussed the idea of marriage and her move to New Orleans in more detail. Jane had professional obligations to conclude in Chicago, as well as finding a new law firm in Louisiana. They gave themselves six months to one year for both the wedding and the move.

After breakfast, they went to Michael's panel session on public policy and minority politics. Jane took an aisle seat to have a good view of her future husband. The panel table had name plates for each speaker. The name plate next to Michael's was Barry Bonds'.

Barry arrived shortly after Michael and the other panelists were seated. As Barry pulled out his chair he whispered in Michael's ear, "Did you hear about Harry Bernstein?"

"No. What about him?" Michael asked.

"He shot himself to death last night in New Orleans." Michael's countenance fell. He tried to pull himself together before it was his turn to speak.

"Next, we have Professors Woods and Bonds from the Institute for Public Policy," said the panel chair. "They have researched the correlation between the number of black elected officials and public policy outcomes."

As Michael began to speak of minority control of city councils and resulting policy outcomes, his attention focused entirely on his subject. "What this analysis suggests," he said, "is that cities in the South, with at least a 25 percent or higher black population, maintain the most aggressive 'minority set-aside' programs compared to cities elsewhere."

After the panel session was completed, the panelists stood up, greeted one another, and mingled with the audience. Barry placed his hand on Michael's shoulder, and said, "You did a good job."

"Thank you," said Michael. "But it's too bad about Bernstein. He was so sure people were out to do him wrong."

"It's a damn shame," said Barry. He turned away to talk to others and quietly left the room.

"That's sad Michael," Jane said that evening at dinner when he told her about Bernstein. "I feel so badly for his family. Sometimes I wonder if all the professional demands are worth it."

Although Jane had never met Bernstein, she felt for him just as Michael did. She assumed he had been overwhelmed by professional demands that he could not measure up to.

"It definitely has me thinking," said Michael. "You work hard and strive to get some place in this world and find that perhaps it's no better than where you came from?"

"What does that say?" Jane wondered. "Be careful what you pray for because you might get it?"

Around nine o'clock that evening Jane dropped Michael off at the hotel. They had decided to call it an early evening. He had a six o'clock flight the next morning and she had a trial to prepare for.

"I'll call you tomorrow night from New Orleans," said Michael before kissing Jane good-bye in the hotel lobby.

"I'll be waiting," responded Jane. "Meanwhile, take care of yourself. I want a healthy husband."

"I will," said Michael, smiling. "Don't you work too hard either."

As Michael was sitting in his hotel room by the window and thinking about Bernstein there was a knock on his door. He got up to answer it.

"Hello Barry."

"Michael. I'm glad you're still up. Hey, have you seen this newspaper article?"

Barry handed Michael a newspaper with a story headlined "Scientists Link Male Sexuality to Gene Theory."

"I believe I saw something on CNN," Michael responded, as he glanced at the story and then sat back down in the chair near the window. "It's not conclusive, though, is it?"

"I'm sure there will be some follow up or replication studies," answered Bonds, seating himself on Michael's bed.

"Aren't you glad this conference is over?" asked Michael, as he began to yawn.

"What this means is that if it's genetic," Bonds asserted, "then governments must expand anti-discrimination laws to the areas of sexual preference. As far as public policy, this places homosexuality in the same category as race and gender." Bonds thought for a second or two and then said, "If it's part of a one's nature, why fight it?"

"Unfortunately, I haven't given the study enough thought to discuss it," wearily replied Michael. "All I can say is that I'm tired and I have an early morning flight. When does your flight leave?"

Michael hoped Bonds would get the subtle hint that he wanted him to leave his hotel room so he tossed the newspaper to the bed where Bonds was sitting. However, when Bonds did not get the hint, Michael stood up and walked towards the bathroom. Bonds, instead of waiting, followed him.

"I still can't get over what happened to Bernstein," said Michael, as he suddenly stopped at the bathroom door with his patience wearing thin. "It'll be a while before I stop seeing his face, pleading with me, to help him."

Bonds brushed off Michael's comments, placed his hand on his own zipper, and stared at Michael.

"What is this about?" demanded Michael, choosing his words carefully. "Is your interest in the story scholarly, personal, or both?"

Bonds said nothing, but his actions suggested that it was more than scholarly, as his stare at Michael grew even more intense.

"I have nothing against the study or the homosexuals," said Michael carefully, his patience wearing thinner. "It's just that I am tired and I don't like people following me when I get up to use the bathroom. I am not gay. But if you wanted to know, a better way was to ask me rather than follow me in here, and stare me down."

Bonds abruptly left Michael's room. Suddenly, Michael realized that he had offended a tenured colleague. He wished it were only an intellectual offense. He could only hope and pray that Bonds would not seek revenge against him.

Chapter Three

Except for an official memo, "recognizing with regrets the untimely death of Harry Bernstein," he was soon forgotten at the Institute. Michael found a copy of the memo in his office mailbox upon his return from the NAPR conference. It was piled in with various other letters.

Things went on as usual. But the memo seemed to take precedence over all Michael's other mail. Sitting at his office desk with the memo in front of him, Michael's eyes focused on the chair where Bernstein had sat, pleading. The memory was overpowering. Michael placed the memo in an empty bottom drawer in his desk. He wanted to save it. Maybe, he thought, he could have helped Bernstein. If he had talked to Bernstein more, could he have prevented him from going over the edge?

Michael knew it was now too late to help Bernstein. But for some reason he felt that if he held onto the memo, he would still have a piece of Bernstein with him. Maybe he was reminding himself not to make the same mistake again. The next time, maybe, if there was a next time, he would not be so self-centered.

At the next faculty meeting, the second week in April, the Institute faculty voted to wait until the fall semester to start recruiting for Bernstein's replacement. It was an emotionless vote. The item was simply listed on the agenda like any other matter. When Mitzie opened it for discussion, Matt Kohl gave her the response she was looking for.

"I don't believe anyone can argue with the fact that it now being mid-April, our ad wouldn't hit the newsletters until the May or June issues," explained Kohl. "We'd basically be recruiting from among left-overs from this past year's searches. I say we wait until the fall and start afresh."

"You're right, Matt," said Barney Holtz. "I move that we put off the search until this fall."

"Second!" said Stan Tullock.

"Any objections?" asked Mitzie. No one objected.

Michael felt sick. No one at the meeting expressed any sympathy whatsoever for Bernstein. In fact, the group of professors who had been friendly with Bernstein, except for Doris, was absent from the meeting. This group included John Walker, Orville Reid, Henry Murphy, and Alex Sanchez. Doris' loyalty was now clear. It was to the powers that be. She was scheduled to come up for promotion and tenure in the fall and would not dare say anything that would cause her superiors to question her loyalty. Michael wanted to say something on Bernstein's behalf, but he did not. He now knew beyond a doubt that those professors who were present hated Bernstein. The only possible exception was Doris, who was in no position to wield any power.

The spring semester came to an end. Michael had completed his first full year as a professor at the Institute. On the whole, his future looked positive. He moved out of his apartment near the campus, and purchased a four-bedroom fixer-upper house in the River Bend section of New Orleans. Michael did most of the work himself, with a little help from his neighbors and friends.

Before he knew it, it was mid-summer and Jane arrived to spend her vacation with him. Although it was summer, many of the professors were still around doing research. Others were teaching summer school.

Michael had briefly mentioned Bernstein's suicide to Jane at the conference in April. However, they had not discussed it since. Nor had he discussed the uneasiness he sometimes felt while at the Institute. Now that Jane was in New Orleans, he finally shared with her the full story. "Organizational politics gone haywire," was Jane's brief response.

It was noon when Jane arrived at Michael's third floor office where they would shortly leave and have lunch together. They chatted and walked down the hallway, stopping briefly to converse with one professor after another. Their last stop was Professor Neuhaus' office.

Jane had heard so many positive things about Doris that she felt she already knew her. As Michael softly tapped on Doris' slightly ajar door, Jane saw the newspaper clippings taped to it. Among the clippings were pictures of neo-Nazis bearing swastikas and robed Ku Klux Klansman carrying Confederate flags. Before she had time to read them all, Doris opened the door and invited them in.

"Hi!" said Doris. "What a surprise. Come on in."

"Hi," said Jane, as she and Michael walked into Doris's office. "It's so good to meet you."

"Well, to be honest," replied Doris, "Michael talks about you all the time."

"He'd better," said Jane.

"Let's have a seat and get better acquainted," suggested Doris, pulling out two chairs from the wall.

"Wish we could," responded Michael, "but we're on our way to lunch. However, I do have a proposition for you."

"What?" curiously responded Doris.

"Jane and I would love it if you and Tyrone could join us for a dinner party at the house tonight. It's at seven o'clock. Can you make it?"

"We'll be there," said Doris, smiling.

"But don't you have to discuss it with Tyrone first?" asked Michael.

"He doesn't have any plans," Doris responded. "We'll be there."

"Bye," said Jane, as she and Michael turned to leave Doris' office.

"See you all tonight," said Doris.

"Looking forward to tonight," said Michael.

"Why does Doris have those Nazi newspaper clippings on her office door?" Jane asked, after she and Michael left the building, got into the car, and started driving to the Garden District, where they would have lunch.

Michael thought for a second or two. "They don't mean anything. Doris is very liberal, like I told you. It's her way of reminding everyone that Duke and Sykes were Nazis before and that they probably still are. She told me that the best way to defeat neo-Nazi propaganda is to challenge it intellectually. That's why she had those guys speak in her classes. I think her exact words were: "Sunshine disinfects and so does the truth."

"Maybe so," said Jane, "But don't you think having that stuff on her door is a little bit spooky?"

"I thought so at first," replied Michael. "But now that I know Doris a little better, I no longer feel that way. Anyway, I thought you two hit it off quite well. Did I miss something?"

"Oh! Don't get me wrong," responded Jane. "I like her and all. I just don't understand the newspaper clippings."

"That's understandable," replied Michael. "But remember, I told you that her boyfriend, Tyrone, is black. They've been seeing each other for a while now."

Later that evening, as Michael and Jane were busy setting the table for their dinner guests, the doorbell rang. It was Doris and Tyrone.

"Hello! Come in!" said Jane. "It's good to see you again."

"Yes, hello again," replied Doris. "I want you to meet Tyrone."

"Pleased to meet you Tyrone. Michael says you're a great tennis player."

"I'm okay. Michael's pretty good too though."

"He's better than he thinks," said Jane.

The doorbell rang again. This time Michael answered it. It was Scott and Beth, their neighbors.

"Doris and Tyrone, meet my neighbors Scott and Beth Harper."

"Hi," said Doris, as she walked over to greet the couple and shake their hands. Tyrone did the same.

"Well, let's all sit down at the table," said Michael.

"Michael, why don't you say the grace," asked Jane.

"Sure," said Michael. "Father, we thank you for the food that is before us for the nourishment of our bodies. And, we thank you for the new found friends that we have invited over. Both are blessings from you. We thank you, Lord. In Jesus' name, Amen."

"We're impressed with both your table and your thankfulness," cheerfully said Beth.

"You guys have really gone out of your way," agreed Scott.

"Well, this is what friends are for," said Michael.

Doris and Jane continued to hit it off, which especially pleased Michael considering he had finally told Jane about the factionalized Institute and answered her questions about Doris' newspaper clippings.

"I was wondering how Chicago is dealing with the death of its mayor," said Scott. "Michael told us that you knew him personally."

"We're coping," said Jane. "It was such a tragedy for the city. And, being that he was the first black mayor - one who had taken on the old machine and won - well, that just made the tragedy all the more terrible."

"I wonder if someone, like a secretary, put something in his coffee that killed him," speculated Tyrone. "You know, they have this stuff now, makes it look like someone's had a heart attack. Doctors can't tell the difference."

"Why do you think that?" asked Michael, looking down the table at Jane.

"Well, everyone knows that the machine hated him," answered Tyrone. What's that guy's name – Bruce Malkovich? I wouldn't be surprised if he was behind it."

"Surely not!" interjected Doris, staring at Tyrone. "Surely not."

Michael thought it was time to change the subject. "On a more positive note," he said. "I want to announce that my first NAPR conference paper has been accepted for publication in the *Western Journal of Public Policy*."

"That's good news," said Tyrone.

"That's great news!" remarked Scott. "What's it about?"

"It's called 'A time series analysis of privatized service delivery in urban America: comparing costs and benefits.' *Western* is not one of the top national journals, but it's a start."

Clearly, Michael's friends were happy for him. But Doris did not seem as enthusiastic as the others. Michael wondered if she was slightly envious.

In the fall after a national search, Mark Vandenberg was offered Bernstein's old job. Vandenberg, fresh out of graduate school at Northwestern, seemed to be a perfect fit with the Institute's power players. As the two youngest faculty members, he and Michael could easily have become friends, but they were simply colleagues who knew each other very little. Vandenberg stayed in his world and Michael stayed in his.

A big part of Michael's responsibilities at the Institute involved outreach to state and local governments. In the process, he got to know Mayor Mitch Deveaux. Mitch was a 35-year-old light skinned, black Creole. His critics said he only became mayor because he inherited the post from his father.

The two first met at the November induction ceremony for new officers of the Orleans Parish Democratic Committee. Michael was there as a guest of his neighbor Scott Harper, who introduced him to the mayor. Scott was one of only two white officers inducted. Weeks later, the mayor invited Michael to come by his office to get better acquainted.

Michael was at first surprised by the amount of attention he received from Mitch. However, he reasoned that ambitious Mitch saw him as a future political asset. He was also well aware that politicians liked the idea of being backed up in their positions by scholars. During that first meeting, Mitch even tossed around the idea of appointing Michael to a couple of city commissions.

Working with the mayor and his staff was rewarding for Michael. The workshops and seminars he conducted were designed around his research expertise. The professional contacts that Michael was developing only added to his sense of confidence at the Institute.

Teaching was definitely third on Michael's list of priorities after research and community service. He did however enjoy teaching graduate students. The seminar in policy implementation, which met once a week at night, was his favorite.

But the undergraduate teaching was a different story. For example, his introduction to American public policy class was filled with academically disinterested students. They complained about the workload and the difficulty of the exams. Many of them were not public policy majors but needed the course to fulfill their own program requirements.

One morning during class, Michael noticed a white student staring at him intently, as if he had offended her. It was the same type of weird stare he had received from David Piston that night at Gator's.

Michael ignored the young woman and continued to lecture. Towards the end of class, he told the class, "I am aware of some of your complaints about the course workload. However, I am not going to reduce the workload. I am not going to do so because I feel the workload is appropriate. However, I want to remind you that you always have the option of dropping this class and taking it later from a less demanding professor."

The following week Michael found a memo in his office mailbox from Mitzie Schultz. It said, "See me ASAP."

"I had a visit from two of your students yesterday," Mitzie told Michael. "It was two young girls. They were in tears and complained to me that you were rude to them in class and refused to answer their questions. Now, I want to hear what you have to say."

It was clear from the look on her face that Mitzie had already sided with the two students. Nothing Michael said would convince her that the allegations were groundless.

"I'm sorry if those two students got that impression of me," he responded quietly. "I'll do my best to become more approachable. Hopefully, they will no longer feel that way."

Gradually, Michael would come to see Mitzie less amicably as she treated him politely in company but rudely when others were not around.

In spite of Mitzie, Michael's excitement about his first article being accepted for publication and his other accomplishments continued to establish his confidence. He submitted two other manuscripts to journals. These included "Public Policy and Black Elected Officials," coauthored with Barry Bonds, and "Privatization and the Impact of Local Political Culture," based on his dissertation research.

Within two months Michael received the journal editors' response to the manuscript he had coauthored with Bonds. The editors of *State Politics Quarterly* requested that the manuscript be revised according to their recommendations and resubmitted for further review. They primarily had problems with the statistical analysis portion of the paper, for which Bonds was responsible, and wanted that portion revised.

But as time went by, Bonds failed to revise this portion of the manuscript. Bonds was already tenured and thus had less to gain from the publication than Michael. Michael decided to go to Mitzie's office, to try to put pressure on Bonds.

"Bonds has decided to no longer work on the project because he feels you are not being an equal partner," sternly replied Mitzie.

Ever since the incident in his Chicago hotel room, Michael had known that Bonds could make life at the Institute difficult for him. Now it seemed that those fears had come true. Several weeks earlier, Michael had asked Barney Holtz for feedback on "Privatization and the Impact of Local Political Culture," before he submitted it to another journal. The manuscript had received only fair reviews on its first submission.

When Holtz returned the manuscript to Michael it was full of remarks indicating that it had nothing new to offer to the field of public policy and was a waste of effort. Michael was crushed. He now had two unpromising manuscripts upon which his career depended. On top of that, his second-year performance review was coming up in two months.

Michael felt that he had no choice but to revise the coauthored piece without Bonds assistance. Three months had gone by since he received the first editorial reviews, and it would take at least two more months to hear from the reviewers again, too late for is second-year review.

While making copies of the manuscript in the main office, Michael noticed a framed document in German, hanging over one of the copy machines.

"What is that?" he asked Gracie Mullen, the head secretary at the Institute.

"That's one of Hitler's speeches," answered Gracie. "*The Fuhrer's Heart*, it's called."

Orville Reid looked up from his mailbox, where he was standing, checking his mail. "It's simply some of that Aryan race garbage," he remarked.

Gracie chuckled.

Other members of the clerical staff laughed in agreement. Reid laughed too. Michael didn't get the joke.

Gradually, Michael's reputation at the Institute had changed. Instead of a prized recruit, he now seemed to be a disappointment. His colleagues appeared to have no confidence in his abilities. He wondered if he was even smart enough to be at the Institute.

This was the first time Michael had entertained such doubts since he had confronted the Greek system back in college. He felt like the little boy from Tutwiler all over again.

One morning that spring, Michael received the response letter from *State Politics Quarterly*. He opened it right away, standing at his mailbox in the Institute's main office. He was filled with jubilation and relief when he saw the letter's first sentence: "Congratulations. Your manuscript entitled 'Black Elected Officials and Public Policy Outcomes,' has been accepted for publication in *State Politics Quarterly*." His coauthored manuscript had been accepted even without Bonds' help. He went down the hall to Mitzie's office.

"Mitzie!" He exclaimed as he walked into the office.

Mitzie looked up with an inquisitive expression on her faced. "Yes. May I help you?"

"I just got this acceptance letter from *State Politics Quarterly*. The manuscript I wrote with Barry has been accepted. I revised it myself without his help, and they accepted it."

"*State Politics Quarterly* is a minor journal," said Mitzie. "It will not change anything." Mitzie then turned away and focused on her computer screen.

Michael was dejected. He was desperate for a publication in what Mitzie considered a major journal. With help from his own research assistant, Mary Schroeder, he revised the manuscript on "Privatization and Local Political Culture," which Holtz had said offered nothing new to the field, and submitted it to *American Journal of Public Policy*, the top journal in the discipline.

Later that week, after his morning class, having returned to his office, he received a telephone call from Mitzie.

"Please come to my office," she said. "Something very important has come up."

Michael had no idea what Mitzie wanted. He hoped it was good news. He hoped that the tenured faculty had reconsidered its evaluation of his publications and was now willing to give him a more positive review. When he arrived in Mitzie's office he saw Stan Tullock there, standing.

"Professor Tullock is here as a witness," Mitzie said to Michael.

"A witness!" inquired Michael. "Why do we need a witness?"

"Just sit down," ordered Mitzie.

Michael was totally without a clue as to what was about to happen. He took a seat. Tullock did the same.

"There are some rumors circulating among the graduate students," Mitzie said, looking directly into Michael eyes, "that you have falsified your research data. It has also been alleged that you engaged your research assistant, Mary Schroeder, to assist you against her will. How do you respond to these most serious allegations against you?"

"What?" Michael felt weary and besieged. "I have absolutely no idea what you are talking about!"

Mitzie and Tullock continued looking directly at Michael. They looked at him as if he were guilty and would crack in a matter of seconds. They seemed to be relishing the moment.

Michael lost his composure. His face grew hot. "They are lying!" Michael shouted. "I'm sick and tired of all these rumors and racist allegations that you've been hearing about me! I am tired of it!"

"We're tired of it, too!" countered Mitzie.

"Yes," said Tullock. "We're tired of hearing all these complaints about you. We cannot dismiss all of them."

Michael stared at Tullock. He wanted to strangle the puny little man with his bare hands. Michael had not been consumed with so much anger since he was eight years old. That's when his stepfather Lucius told young Philip to beat him up in front of a group of adult relatives and neighbors who chose to do nothing. Philip was Michael's classmate and Lucius's nephew. Michael re-lived the torment within a split second. Now, Michael hated Tullock the way he hated Lucius back then.

While Tullock was talking, Mitzie momentarily glanced away from Michael, but after Tullock finished speaking, her eyes turned back to Michael. "Racism is a very serious charge," she declared. "You'd better be able to back up that kind of allegation before you start lashing out at people!"

"I suggest we conduct a thorough investigation to determine who is telling the truth here," said Tullock.

As Michael left the office, his face showed extreme disappointment. His liberal colleagues would not believe him. Why did the unsubstantiated word of some graduate student carry more weight than his own?

Michael thought he had maintained a very cordial relationship with Mary Schroeder, his research assistant. He assumed he could call her and resolve the situation before Mitzie and Tullock formalized their investigation. He was sure that Mary would say that it had all been a misunderstanding. He felt sure that if Mary knew who had started the rumor, she would tell him and that would resolve the problem. But when Michael called Mary on the telephone, he was surprised to find her response.

"Well, that's not how I understood it, Dr. Woods," Mary said. "I felt that you were forcing me to engage in what I thought could be unethical data coding."

Michael's face tightened. "Mary! I can't believe this. I would never force you to do anything like that. If you questioned my directions why didn't you say something?"

"I did!" responded a determined Mary.

"No! You did not!" exclaimed Michael. "I cannot believe this! You are just giving these people something to use against me! You are just a white racist!" Michael hung up the telephone.

It was his word against Mary Schroeder's, and Mitzie and Tullock already believed Schroeder. After all, what did Schroeder have to gain by lying? Nothing. What did Michael have to gain by lying? Promotion and tenure.

Sitting in his office, Michael prayed: "Lord. Please let this problem be quickly resolved. Please." But his prayer was not answered. Later in the week, he received a letter in his office mailbox from Mitzie, stating that Mary Schroeder had filed an official grievance against him claiming that he "used vile and obscene language to her over the telephone and called her 'a racist bitch.'"

Michael immediately went to Mitzie's office to deny Mary's allegations. "I did not do this," he said. "This is wrong."

"You can be fired for intimidating a student," replied Mitzie.

"I intimidated no one!" Michael exclaimed. "She is lying! I called her no such thing! I am under attack here!"

"You can tell that to the university-wide grievance committee," Mitzie said to Michael. "Now, excuse me. I have work to do."

Michael found himself in a situation that he thought he would never be in. How could this have happened? Now, it seemed as if all of his efforts had been in vain. Everyone had let him down. God was not answering his prayers. However, Michael vowed that he would not go down without a fight.

He decided to file a grievance with the university administration against the Institute for Public Policy. In it, he wrote that the Institute harbored a climate of racism. He claimed that this climate of racism prevented him from receiving fair evaluations from both students and faculty.

This was what the Institute had been waiting for. In a formal response to Michael's claims, Mitzie produced written copies of the allegations from the "two young girls" who had said Michael was rude and unapproachable as a professor. She also produced an additional list of anonymous student complaints which she provided to the grievance committee but refused to allow Michael to see.

In April, one week before the formal grievance hearings were to begin, Michael again went to Mitzie's office, in a last-ditch effort to appeal to her sense of fairness, if she had any. His intentions were good.

"Mitzie, I need to talk to you. I want to resolve these problems amicably, if possible."

Mitzie's face was strained, but she did not interrupt him.

"I do feel that there is a climate of racism here at the Institute. Maybe the Institute leadership is not aware of it because you have never had a black professor before. But it is my perception that students do not give me the same level of respect that they give to white junior professors. And, I believe that it's a reflection of how they see the faculty treating me. In other words, if the faculty encouraged the graduate students to have me on their committees, the students would feel that the faculty respected my capabilities and give me the same respect they give other professors."

Mitzie's face did not soften.

"I'm sorry, she said. "These student grievances deserve to be heard. You should know that we've been down this road before. We always win. We're not anti-Semitic and we're not racist. I think I speak for the entire faculty when I say that we are insulted by your claims. In other words, you have cast the die, and you must suffer the consequences."

"This is harassment!" Michael shouted loudly.

Matt Kohl, Barney Holtz, and Stan Tullock were standing in the hallway near Mitzie's door. "This type of behavior will not be tolerated at the Institute," Kohl asserted. "The time has passed to do something about Woods."

"He has been a troublemaker since the day he arrived here," said Barney Holtz. "He's alleging racism to cover up his performance. It's like having Bernstein all over again."

"If you believe him, there is a racist behind every bush," said Stan Tullock. "Unfortunately, he didn't live up to the promising start. But, we tried."

"Yes, we did," said Kohl. "And someone we tried to help is now calling us racists. I knew it would come to this."

Some of the other professors, hearing Michael's outburst, came to their doors to see what was going on. As Michael walked down the hallway, he realized from the looks on their faces that he had been demonized. The lone exception was John Walker, who looked at Michael as if he pitied him but could not help him.

The special committee appointed by Mitzie to look into the graduate student allegations met in the Institute conference room later that same day. The committee consisted of three Institute faculty members, including Stan Tullock, who thoroughly went over Michael's data analysis and raw data.

"Well, the raw data suggest there was no inappropriate use or falsification," said committee chair Elliott Nussmeyer.

"Let me look at that one last time," said Stan Tullock. "We have to be absolutely sure before we make our recommendation to Mitzie. Tullock pored over the computer printout of Michael's raw data and compared them to the regression models used in Michael's manuscript. "Well, Mary Schroeder was justified in wanting a fuller explanation as to why he had her code the data this way. I can see how it would be confusing to her. He's at fault for not doing that. But, you're right. We wouldn't prevail on this in a university-wide committee." Tullock scratched his head.

"Good," said Orville Reid. "Let's get our final conclusion to the Director immediately. "I am sure Michael will be glad to get this news."

Nussmeyer went down to Mitzie's office and shared the information with her. "I'm sorry, Mitizie. I know you were counting on this to help the Institute in countering Woods' claims of racism. But, there is no way we could prevail at the university level. We'd lose."

"That's okay," said Mitzie. "We may not need that. Mary Schroeder's letter of complaint against him may be enough. No matter how much he shouts racism, nothing will excuse his calling a student a bitch. We can fire him over that."

The university-wide grievance committee met on three separate days, April 14, 15, and 17. The hearings were held in the university administration building, down the hall from the president's office. The committee heard each witness separately. Michael was the first witness to speak to the committee. He spoke on April 14. Committee members, sitting around a rectangular conference table, first introduced themselves and then stated their departmental affiliations. After the introductions were completed the grievance committee chair, College of Business Professor Joe Ruter, said to Michael, "So, let's hear what you have to say."

"Well, I want you all to know," said Michael, "that I have done my best to be a collegial member of the Institute for Public Policy. I have done my best to meet Institute requirements in teaching, research, and service. And, I believe I have met those requirements in all instances and exceeded them in others.

"However, I believe that there is an orchestrated effort to undermine my professional credibility." Michael paused and then said, "I believe this is being done because of my race."

Committee members listened. Michael took a computer printout from his attaché case and said, "Here. Here is proof that I never fabricated any research data."

"No one is claiming that you did at this point," said Bill Jones, a committee member from the Department of Anthropology. "Your director has gone on record with that."

"But it's these allegations that have created all the tension," responded Michael.

"Maybe it's how you responded to the allegations," stated Ruter.

"I disagree," said Michael, "I disagree because these are the worst types of allegations one can make against a professor. Allegations of falsifying data and verbally abusing students demand a loud and clear response, especially when they are groundless. You have to believe that my response to these allegations was justified. I was only defending myself! Just as I falsified no research data, I also used no vile or abusive language toward any student. I did no such thing."

"Well, what did you say to her?" asked Annabel Lopez, a committee member from the Department of Romance Languages.

"I called her a white racist," said Michael. "But, I did so only after it was evident that she was deliberately accusing me of falsifying data, an accusation which you now know is not true."

Annabel, a native of Ecuador, did not like Michael. Michael sensed it. He also knew that the administration had her on the committee to claim that it had minority representation. But as far as Michael was concerned, Annabel was just another white woman. Although Michael had little interaction with Hispanics, he could tell that Annabel was striving to be more white than the other whites on the committee. It was all revealed in her tone of voice. It was all revealed in the manner in which Annabel spoke to Michael in her Spanish accent.

"These allegations against me," Michael concluded, "were orchestrated for one purpose. They were born out of a climate of racism. Racism that exists at the so-called liberal Institute for Public Policy."

Few of the grievance committee members seemed to sympathize with Michael. He sensed that the majority were on the verge of being openly hostile to him.

Mitzie appeared before the grievance committee on Tuesday, the next day. "He is a loose cannon," she told the committee members. "Matt Kohl warned Michael Woods several times about his anger. The Institute has done its best to reason with him. But we are sorry to say that noting seems to work."

Mitzie then looked at the committee members and said, "He has verbally assaulted me on more than one occasion. In addition, I am constantly bombarded with complaints from students who claim that he is rude, antagonistic, and hostile towards them in the classroom."

"I've heard that he has a history of being a trouble maker," said Joe Ruter. "Sources tell us that he was like that before he came here."

"It's definitely patterned behavior," responded Mitzie. "But finally, I want you to know beyond any doubt that Michael Woods has failed to meet organizational requirements as stipulated in his contract. He has published in no major journals and his teaching is obviously substandard. He is simply alleging racism to cover up his shortcomings."

Two days later, an obviously shaken Mary Schroeder appeared before the grievance committee with her husband, Dane. She told the committee that she was nervous and wanted her husband there with her. The committee allowed him to stay.

"What exactly did Professor Woods say to you, hon?" asked committee member Barbara O'Patrick, an English professor who grew up in a small Mississippi town, and in her slow Southern drawl.

In her response, Mary almost began to cry. However, Dane put his arm around her. He comforted her. "C'mon honey," he said, "I'm here with you."

Mary sucked her tears back in. "I was just so afraid," she then told the committee. "I simply told him that I did feel pressured. I only wanted to find out for myself whether the coding was correct." Mary paused and then said, "It's just that no one has ever said things like that to me before." She looked around the conference table and said, "He told me he'd knock my fucking white head off my body if I didn't stop lying on him. 'I'll do it,' he said, 'cause that's what lying, racist bitches deserve.'"

Mary then began to cry, as husband Dane consoled her. The committee bought Mary's story hook, line and sinker.

"Thank you for coming here today," said committee chair and business school professor Joe Ruter. "You've made our job a whole lot easier."

"We're sorry you had to go through this experience with a professor who is supposed to be a role model for students," said Annabel Lopez. "But, things will get better. You just hang in there."

Several of the committee members, including Lopez and O'Patrick, gave Mary a hug. Others shook Dane's hand before he and Mary left the conference room.

"Well, President Hodge Williams told us this is the way we'd decide, and he was right," Ruter said to the committee.

"Let's get it over with," responded O'Patrick.

Ruter passed out ballots with option "A" favoring Professor Woods and option "B" favoring the Institute and Mary Schroeder. Option "B" won unanimously.

Mary Schroeder's testimony and the collaborating evidence provided to the committee by Mitzie Schultz led to the ruling that Michael had failed to satisfy the requirements of the Institute by his demonstration of hostile conduct towards students and faculty.

The grievance committee also agreed with Mitzie that Michael failed to satisfy Institute requirements in the area of publication. His failure in the area of teaching was substantiated according to the committee, based upon the number of student complaints against him. It did not matter to the committee that Michael never saw any of the other alleged student complaints which Mitzie claimed she had.

Afterwards, the Institute's tenured faculty recommended that Michael's contract not be renewed. That gave him one more year at the Institute. He was in the second year of a signed three-year contract, and it was almost impossible to force him out early. The recommendation was approved at every level of the administrative hierarchy, all the way up the president of the university.

Chapter Four

Michael's six-year tenure track position was no more. He had one year left at the Institute with no possibility of renewal. Now, several professors who were not associated with the Institute attempted to come to his defense. A history professor, Erroll Fontenot, telephoned Michael at home after hearing about the university's decision.

"I'm sorry to hear that the university has decided to go along with your Institute's recommendation regarding non-renewal of your contract," Fontenot said to Michael. "The Black Faculty and Staff Association is having a meeting Thursday morning at nine o'clock. We invite you to come and apprise us of your situation. At that time, we can decide whether or not it is appropriate for us to take a position regarding the decision. Will you come?"

"Sure," said Michael. "I don't feel like talking right now but I will be there Thursday morning. Thanks for calling."

Members of the group were impressed when they saw Michael's curriculum vitae.

"I cannot believe that a black professor with publications like this would not get his contract renewed," said Psychology Professor Carol Sweeney.

"I did not call anyone a bitch," Michael told the group. "I do not use that kind of language. What I called her was a white racist."

"And that's what she is," agreed Sweeney. "This place just makes me sick."

"We all have to take our antidotes before coming to work at these white universities," explained Fontenot. "They never give a black man any credit for what he does."

"Yeah, we have to be twice as damn good and then never open our damn mouth about anything. If we do, we're just trouble makers," said Sweeney. "What are we going to do? Erroll, as president, are you going to meet with Calabrese?"

"In order to demand a meeting, we must be able to present Calabrese with some easy options," answered Fontenot. "Professor Woods' degree in public policy qualifies him to teach in the School of Urban Studies."

Fontenot then looked at Edna Auta, a professor from Urban Studies. "What's the sentiment over there, Edna? Have you heard any talk one way or the other about Woods?"

"I haven't heard anything," responded Auta. "I don't see why Hebert would object. That is, unless politics gets in the way."

"You can never dismiss politics at this place," said Sweeney, throwing her arms into the air.

"Why don't I talk to Dean Hebert and see if he'd be agreeable to having Professor Woods' line transferred to Urban Studies?" asked Fontenot.

"That sounds good to me," said Michael.

"First," said Fontenot, "let's take a vote. We need to follow our rules."

The seven professors and ten staff members who were present voted unanimously to have their president approach Calabrese but only if Hebert agreed to support a line transfer. After the meeting the professors and staff members shook Michael's hand. Of the 2,000 professors at Orleans University, only 11 were black. The bulk of the Black Faculty and Staff Association's membership consisted of staff, which meant that if the organization had any influence, it was strictly symbolic. "I'm going right to my office and see if I can get Hebert to have lunch with me," Fontenot said to Michael, as he shook his hand. "Why don't you come with me?"

Back at the History Department, Fontenot called Hebert from his office. Michael stood in front of Fontenot's desk, listening to Fontenot make the lunch date at the University Club.

When Michael and Fontenot entered the University Club dining area at eleven thirty, they found Dean Hebert there, already seated. "Dean," said Fontenot, as he and Michael walked up to the table, "this is Professor Michael Woods from the Institute for Public Policy."

"Oh yes, I've met Professor Woods on several occasions. Will you be joining us, Michael?"

"Yes," said Michael.

"Well, please have a seat."

"So," said Dean Hebert to Fontenot, as Fontenot and Michael were sitting down, "what's so important that you had to see me ASAP?"

"Are you familiar with the grievance committee's recommendation regarding Michael Woods?"

"Yes. I am," said Hebert. "It was unfortunate. Professor Woods and I have talked on several occasions and I must say to you, Michael, that I am sorry."

"Thanks," said Michael.

"What do you think about the idea of having Professor Woods join the School of Urban Studies?" asked Fontenot.

"The School of Urban Studies could use someone with Professor Woods' background in urban policy. However, first I'd like to know how Calabrese and Hodge Williams come down on this."

"We don't know that yet," responded Fontenot. "However, the Black Faculty and Staff Association voted this morning to lobby for the transfer if we can secure your backing ahead of time. If you give me the thumbs up, I will leave here and immediately demand a meeting with Calabrese for this afternoon."

Hebert turned and looked at Michael. "As I said, we have met and talked on a number of occasions and you don't strike me as hostile in the least. If the provost lets it happen, I'd have no objection to having you join us. It would be to our benefit." Hebert then looked at Fontenot. "You can tell Calabrese that I'm for it."

"Well, this is going to be a good lunch," said Fontenot.

Michael smiled.

After lunch, Fontenot had his secretary set up a four o'clock meeting with the provost. Michael went back to his office and closed the door. He did not want to face the people at the Institute.

His telephone rang. "Michael, this is Erroll. I just confirmed a four o'clock meeting with Calabrese. This is what I think we should do. I want you to be at my office at 3:45. Can you be here?"

"Yes."

"Okay. I want you to walk over to the provost office with me. However, I think that only I should go in and talk to Calabrese. Is that okay?"

"That's okay."

"Okay, if he hints that he is willing to carry your torch, I'll tell him that you're outside and would like to talk to him. Otherwise, it's best that I try to convince him on my own. Who knows? A little pressure from the Black Faculty and Staff Association just might move him."

Fontenot's optimism was contagious. Suddenly, the day's events had Michael feeling positive once again. If he could escape from the Institute and move to the School of Urban Studies, it would prevent any interruption in his career. Just as importantly, he would still have a job. And, the frightening thought of not being able to make his large mortgage payments would be just that, a thought.

Fontenot's cheerful demeanor suggested that the transfer was a done deal. Michael could not allow himself to be that upbeat. Rather, cautious optimism was what he felt at 3:30 p.m. after being locked in his office for three hours. That's when he finally opened his office door and left the Institute building to avoid seeing anyone. Cautious optimism continued to describe his frame of mind as he entered Fontenot's office and walked with Fontenot over to the Office of the Provost.

"Wait here," Fontenot said to Michael, as he walked confidently into Calabrese's office.

"I thought it was only a matter of time before you showed up," said Calabrese, sitting behind his desk, looking relaxed. "So, what do you have to say?"

"We feel that Professor Woods deserves another chance," said Fontenot. "There have been rumors for some time now that something smells at that Institute."

"There are always rumors circulating when people don't get their way," responded Calabrese. His relaxed posture began to tighten. "The Institute has a sound civil rights reputation. The professors there are responsible for some of the cutting-edge research on civil rights policy. Allegations of racism, like those argued by Woods, just don't hold water."

"I talked to the dean of the School of Urban Studies," responded Fontenot. "He expressed a willingness to bring Woods in. All you have to do is transfer his line from that Institute over to Urban Studies. You just have to do it before Professor Woods' contract expires next year. I am asking you to do this because we need more black professors here. Woods has published. I think he's a good professor. I don't think this university can afford to lose him."

"He's accused of intimidating and threatening bodily injury to a student," countered Calabrese. "He's accused of hostile behavior towards his superiors. That doesn't sound like a good professor to me. He sounds like the kind of professor this university would be better off without."

"Dr. Calabrese, there is absolutely no doubt in my mind that if Woods had been in the history department rather than the Institute of Public Policy, he'd still have a job. I'd go as far as to say that with his publication record, he'd be on his way to promotion and tenure."

"His non-collegiality aside," said Calabrese, "it's not up to me to tell you whether your standards in history are below par. That's up to your dean. But, speaking from this end, comparing the history department to the Institute for Public Policy is like comparing apples and oranges. Your department is not in the same league."

"I will ignore that comment," said Fontenot, "because there is a more important issue before us. Perhaps it's not Woods who is bad. Perhaps it is the Institute. We have no way of knowing. We have no way of knowing whether or not the all white grievance committee's recommendation was a fair one. But what we do know is that the last thing this university needs is a race discrimination lawsuit."

"Wait one minute!" said Calabrese. "That situation was investigated, may I say, by an impartial, university-wide grievance committee. All of Woods' allegations were discounted. On the other hand, all allegations against him were deemed plausible and accurate."

"You had one, young, black assistant professor going up against an entrenched institution here at this university," said Fontenot. "All I am saying is, if there are other departments on this campus where he would be a better fit, this university's commitment to racial diversity and affirmative action demands that he be given every opportunity to go there."

"Well," said Calabrese, "the School of Urban Studies has tenured two black professors over the past 20 years and the Institute has tenured none. Four years ago, the Institute was one of six university units which had no black faculty at all. That's why the administration put pressure on the Institute to hire an African American. The people over there promised that they would go after and get the top black PhD graduate in the country. And, the university gave them the necessary funds to proceed. In other words, Fontenot, the Institute made good on its promise. We cannot fault them, for Woods' failure."

Fontenot opened his briefcase, pulled out a sheet of paper, and handed it to Calabrese. "Here Dr. Calabrese. Here is a petition. It is signed by members of the university's Black Faculty and Staff Association. We want your office to investigate all possibilities of transferring Professor Woods to the School of Urban Studies. That's all I have to say."

Fontenot got up without making any additional eye contact with Calabrese and walked to the door. As he opened the door, he turned around and looked Calabrese in the face. "Oh, by the way, it was a pleasure talking to you."

Fontenot had been optimistic before his meeting with Calabrese, but Calabrese's arrogance had made him angry. He and the other black faculty had long detested the arrogance of the all-white Institute for Public Policy, which considered itself too good to hire black professors.

Fontenot recalled the words of the Institute's Faculty Senate representative, Elliott Nussmeyer. "Our standards are so much higher than that of other university units. Thus, it is very difficult for us to find a black PhD with an adequate level of training to succeed at such a high caliber research Institute as ours." These were the words ringing in Fontenot's ears as he left Calabrese's office. He could see Nussmeyer's pudgy face as he had said those words in a faculty senate meeting three years earlier.

Michael's situation was a convenient tool for the Black Faculty and Staff Association to use to take another jab at the Institute. If Calabrese had allowed the transfer to take place, it would have been the same as Michael winning his grievance in that the Institute's evaluation of Michael would have been mooted by the university administration.

That is exactly what Fontenot and his association wanted: a blow to the face of the high and mighty Institute.

The association's animosity toward the Institute was much older than the two years Michael had spent at Orleans. Michael did not know that the Black Faculty and Staff Association had long detested the Institute. He thought the Association was simply upset because of how the Institute had treated him.

"I'm sorry Michael," said Fontenot, as he walked up to Michael, who was still sitting in the waiting area. Michael stood up.

"So, it didn't go that well, hah?"

"No, it didn't," said Fontenot. "He didn't give me a slam-in-my-face no. But, it was a no nonetheless. It was clearly more no than it was yes. To be honest with you, I'll be surprised if he does anything. You should start looking for another job."

"Well, you tried," said Michael as he and Fontenot walked out of the administration building. "To be honest with you, I knew nothing would come of this. The Institute wields too much power with Hodge Williams. Calabrese knows that. I guess I just wanted to hold onto any faint hope that I may have had."

Michael the next day received his official termination letter. The letter from Mitzie simply stated, "This is to inform you that your contract will not be renewed beyond the 1989-90 academic year."

Although Michael anticipated the news, the reality of the letter threw him into an emotional tailspin, but he was determined not to let it show. As he walked down the hallway toward his office, he held the letter in his hand. Out of the corner of his eye, Michael saw two male graduate students down the hall. One was white with brown hair and one was fat and black with thick eye glasses. The fat one was the only black graduate student at the Institute although he had never taken a class from Michael. The two students giggled and then quickly dashed into Barry Bonds' office.

Michael didn't have the heart for the crucial meeting he had scheduled later that afternoon with Mayor Mitch Deveaux, but he decided that the meeting was too important to cancel. He arrived at the mayor's office at three o'clock. Michael did his best to assume his normal talkative rapport with Mitch, but he could tell that Mitch realized something was wrong. Mitch became less businesslike. He propped his feet on his desk and started to talk about non-policy issues.

"You know," he said, his black wingtips on top of his desk, "I'm thinking of running for that new congressional seat if it gets approved. That's a $90,000 a year job. Being mayor pays good too, but my family and I think I should be in Washington. That's where my future is."

"Washington, hah?" responded Michael.

"Yeah, "said Mitch." I've pretty much carried on my father's legacy here in New Orleans. I probably wouldn't have even run for mayor if he had lived."

"He did great things for blacks in this city," responded Michael.

Michael saw Mitch shake his face as if he were shaking off thoughts of his father. He changed the subject back to himself. "Washington - that's what I'm setting my sights on next."

"That's good," said Michael. "One thing about elective politics is that you don't have white bias evaluating your performance. When you're elected by a black majority, you don't have to worry about that."

Michael saw Mitch sensing that he was having trouble at the Institute, but Mitch avoided asking direct questions about it.

"You right about that, brother," said Mitch, standing up as if he were about to preach a sermon. "It's like the professional basketball player. No one can discount their talent. No one can argue with it, because they show it on the court. If the white man could subjectively evaluate basketball player performance, we'd have mostly white players in the

NBA. Any occupation out there where our talent can be shown - shown without the interaction effect of white bias - our brilliance always shines through."

"That's pretty good," said Michael, looking up at Mitch.

"Whites will never give us blacks credit for what we deserve!" said Mitch, as he tightened his fists and preached. "We have to take it! I tell you, brother, I couldn't work for them. My personality is too strong! It's good my father left me this legacy. I'm fortunate."

"You are," said Michael. "Indeed, you are."

Michael needed help, but he dared not mention his situation to Mitch, who was a lot of talk and not much else. In addition, Michael knew Mitch was tight with Hodge Williams. Michael also knew that Matt Kohl had built a multi-million-dollar consulting business through the contacts he had made through Mitch's father when he was mayor. Matt Kohl was a senior political advisor to Mitch. Michael knew that Mitch would not dare endanger his Hodge Williams connections or his connections with the Institute for Public Policy. Mitch, Michael knew, was a politician who lived by political gain. So, Michael did not share his pain. He swallowed it instead.

"Well, it's three-thirty and I've got to be somewhere at four," Mitch said suddenly. Michael stood up and Mitch quickly escorted him to the door.

"Nice seeing you again, Dr. Woods," said Mitch's flirtatious secretary.

"Nice seeing again, too, Shirley," Michael replied.

"I'm glad you came," said Mitch. "I enjoyed the talk. We can take up that planning issue next time."

"Thanks," responded Michael, "I enjoyed it too."

Michael left Mitch's office feeling empty. He wanted something from Mitch that he knew Mitch could not or would not give. He wanted support. He couldn't blame Mitch, though, he had not told him what had happened at the Institute. Deep down inside, Michael knew that it was best that way.

In the long run, Michael only hoped that his positive working relationship with the mayor would not be tarnished by the Institute's judgment of him. But before long Mitch learned of Michael's misfortune, and after that, Michael's relationship with the mayor gradually declined. Michael's phone calls were returned less frequently. The secretary told him that the mayor was busy. And finally, City Hall stopped calling Michael to arrange for the outreach sessions. The cold shoulder treatment continued even after Michael sent Mitch a certified letter fully briefing him on what actually happened.

About a month later, in May, it all began to hit Michael like a cannon ball. He had never felt so wronged, so helpless, so destitute, so betrayed in his entire life. This was worse than the torment he had experienced as a child back in Tutwiler. It was worse because his position at the Institute was something that he had worked hard to achieve. Now, it had been snatched away just as he had begun to taste its goodness. He hadn't even had time to savor its sweet flavor before that flavor turned bitter as wormwood. This was the greatest wrong Michael ever encountered. For the first time, he began to hate white people.

May was also the month Michael flew back to Tutwiler to comfort his mother when Lucius died. After years of smoking and drinking, Lucius had been stricken with throat and lung cancer. Michael felt no loss, but he knew he had to be there for his mother and his younger brother Steve.

Michael was solemn during the funeral services and throughout his brief stay in Tutwiler. His solemnity had nothing to do with Lucius.

After the funeral, a host of Lucius' relatives came to the house trailer with covered dishes. Relatives of Michael's mother did the same. They sat at the kitchen table. They sat in the living room. They sat where ever they could find a seat. They talked. They ate. They comforted. Miss Colleen, the mother of Philip and the sister of Lucius, was there. Miss Faye was also there. She was Lucius's niece. They were in the midst of these people, talking and eating. So were Aunt Jerrie and Aunt Mary, along with their children and grandchildren.

Realizing that his mother could now spare him for a while, Michael left the crowded house and drove his rental car to a Richmond shopping mall. He found the peace and quiet of walking among strangers soothing.

After a couple of hours, he drove back to Tutwiler to find the house almost empty of visitors. He was not ready to go in, though, and instead, he walked down the hill to his grandmother's house.

"C'mone in," said Grandma, as she opened the door. "How's my grandson the professor doing?" Grandma then walked back into her bedroom and climbed up on her bed. She was not sick. Grandma just preferred to spend most of her time in her bedroom. She liked to sit up in bed and read the Bible, day and night. Michael followed her into the bedroom. "Have a seat somewhere and tell me how you been doing."

"I'm fine, Grandma," Michael responded. He sat in the chair across the room. Grandma had a Bible on her nightstand. It was opened to where she had been reading. It was opened to the Book of James, where she had been reading.

"I don't go to funerals, you know," said Grandma. "I can't take them. How's your Mama holding up?"

"She's doing okay, I guess. I just wanted to come and visit you for a while. I'm going back tomorrow morning."

"Well! I'm glad you came to see me. You know I'm always glad to see my grandson the professor."

Grandma and the other family members were proud of Michael. They constantly bragged about his accomplishments to others in the town. This did not make Michael's dilemma any easier. After visiting his grandmother, Michael spent a quiet evening with his mother and brother. He flew back to New Orleans the next day.

Michael knew he could no longer avoid informing his fiancé about his situation. He had postponed telling her in the hope that the grievance committee would find in his favor.

He started the telephone conversation by discussing his trip to Tutwiler and Lucius' funeral. He then shifted the conversation entirely to a different subject.

"Jane, I wonder why it is that bad things always seem to happen to good people?"

"What do you mean?" Jane asked.

"I mean people like me. I have been holding off on telling you something for a while. I hoped things would turn out differently so I would not have to tell you. But I don't guess I can wait any longer."

"Tell me what? You're not sick, are you?" nervously asked Jane.

"No. I'm not sick. I just was not renewed at the Institute."

Michael then went into detail and explained the accusations of Mary Schroeder and how they resulted in grievances being filed and his losing. Jane was supportive. They talked for hours.

Afterwards, Michael called his mother. He had not mentioned his troubles to her because of the more pressing family loss. However, she had made him promise long ago to never keep anything important from her. In the midst of informing his mother about his problems at the Institute Michael abruptly said to her, "I hate white people! I hate them for what they've done to me!"

"Harboring hatred will only eat you alive," was Pearl's immediate response. "If you want to overcome this, you must be strong, think clearly, and pray for those enemies of yours. If you do that, God will bless you in return."

That night, Michael fell down on his knees and cried out to God. "Oh, heavenly father, please guide me in dealing with this matter in the appropriate way. I need you father. Bless those who curse and spitefully use me."

With tears in his eyes, Michael thanked God for his mother, and asked God's blessings upon her. His feelings of hatred began to subside.

Chapter Five

During the summer Michael and Jane contacted a New Orleans attorney who agreed to take his case on a contingency basis. Michael had unsuccessfully contacted three other attorneys on his own but they had all refused him.

He was happy with Barbara Tisdale. In addition to being one of the city's most successful civil litigators, Tisdale had connections with Jane's Chicago law firm. Michael believed that connection played a key role in her deciding to take his case.

"I am truly disappointed in the attorneys who turned me down," Michael told Tisdale. "Jane and I believe they did so because of the local civil rights community's ties to the Institute. What do you think?"

"Unfortunately, the two of you may be onto something," responded Tisdale. "Life is no utopia. There is no Perry Mason. And yes, the Institute and local civil rights leaders have been in bed together for the past decade."

A tall woman with a hearty personality, Tisdale was a 41-year-old Yale Law School graduate who had never married. "I grew up in North Louisiana," she said. "I guess that allows me to consider myself an outsider."

"How long have you been practicing in New Orleans?" asked Michael.

"Ten years," said Tisdale. "I left one of the city's biggest law firms five years ago to go off on my own."

"And you've definitely done quite well for yourself," remarked Jane.

"I do okay," said Tisdale, smiling. "Getting back to your question about the other attorneys who turned you down, most black attorneys here are under contract with the university because of the Institute's role in civil rights policy." Tisdale's smile then began to fade. "The local NAACP is at the center of it. I advise you to not even approach the NAACP. The local chapter is less than a paper tiger. They will not oppose their influential white supporters."

"You know it hurts me," responded Michael, "to think that the organization that is supposed to define racial equality, an organization I have held dear to my heart my whole life, doesn't care what happens to me."

"It's not that they don't care," responded Tisdale. "It's simply that money buys influence. Always has. Always will. Because much of their monetary support comes from the white liberal establishment, they are in essence controlled by it."

"It's that bad?" asked Jane.

"That's right," replied Tisdale. "No member of the civil rights community exemplifies that more than local NAACP president, Russell Brown. He has close ties not only to the Institute but also to university President Hodge Williams.

"Oh my! Williams is such a polished, Boss Hogg type," declared Jane.

Michael, Jane, and Tisdale all chuckled.

"So, Russ Brown, the 47-year-old bald guy, is known as a consummate beggar for white money?" asked Michael.

"Yes," responded Tisdale. "But you know he was really instrumental, along with the state chapter, in getting that new black majority congressional district approved. So, now we'll have two black congressmen."

"Is there anything else we need to be doing?" Jane asked Tisdale.

"There's nothing more that can be done right now," responded Tisdale. "I'll file this petition this afternoon. Hopefully, the defendants will all be served later this week. What we do now is wait for their response. It's my bet that they will attempt to cast Michael as a ticking time bomb or as a loose cannon. It's easy for whites to portray black men that way. They even did it at the grievance committee stage. I expect they'll continue hammering on it."

"Well, you don't know how much I appreciate your agreeing to take my case," said Michael. "You know how to reach me when the time comes."

As Tisdale stood up so did Michael and Jane. "I'll be in touch," said Tisdale as she shook Michael's hand. "If the past is any indication, we can expect a trial date within a year."

"It was nice to finally meet you," said Jane as she too shook Tisdale's hand. "Goodbye."

"Until later," said Tisdale.

The following day, Tisdale watched the evening news in her conference room. It was six o'clock and she was alone in the office. She wanted to see the local reaction to the creation of the new black congressional district. Much to her surprise, the news reporter asked Russ Brown, "What's your reaction to the racial discrimination lawsuit recently filed against Hodge Williams, the Institute of Public Policy, and Orleans University."

"We should not expect anything we haven't earned," answered Russ Brown. Hodge Williams' record on civil rights is clear. You cannot have a better example than his Institute's support for the creation of this new black majority district."

"You bastard!" said Tisdale, standing up in disgust. "I will definitely save this one!" Tisdale collected video-taped newscasts. They often came in handy during court trials. She was now torn between appreciation for Russ Brown's role in creating the new congressional district and anger at his statements regarding her client.

The reporter, a white woman, went on. "White conservatives welcome the new black district majority because it allows Louisiana's white congressmen to represent whiter districts, freeing them of black concerns at reelection time as well as during congressional voting."

A black man whose name Barbara Tisdale didn't catch, stated, "The new district is just a new approach to diluting black votes. It's relabeled and repackaged but it's still the same thing. That is, blacks will come up at the short end on crucial congressional voting."

Tisdale, Democrat, disagreed. Like her friends at the Orleans Parish Democratic Committee, she felt that physical representation was more important because blacks had been denied it much too long.

In the ensuing months, Jane increased the frequency of her weekend visits to New Orleans. After dinner one evening, she and Michael turned on the television, and snuggled up on the sofa, to watch the local news. Is that the guy you work with?" asked Jane.

"Yes, that's Matt Kohl," said Michael. "I don't believe this! The state NAACP is giving him an award for the citizen who contributed the most to the progress of blacks last year."

"The award," said the black female news anchor, "is based on Dr. Kohl's work in the development of the new black majority congressional district." Adding, "Critics say its creation has made other districts whiter, and have vowed to challenge it in the courts."

"That's tough," said Jane. Unfortunately, I can see both sides."

Michael had never felt so low. On the coffee table in front of him was the tape Barbara Tisdale had given him showing Russ Brown's public declaration of the Institute's innocence. Now, Matt Kohl was receiving a commendation from the civil rights community.

"You know Jane, our wedding can't take place this August. It's already June, and there's just no way we can go through with this, things being what they are."

"But why put off the wedding? We'll pull through this. Michael! I love you. This wedding may be just the thing to put some sanity back into our lives."

"Jane, the last thing I want is to muddy something as beautiful as our marriage vows in the quagmire that I'm in. What if the strain of the court battle is too much for our relationship? What if I don't find another job? What will that do to the marriage?"

"If we love each other, our love will withstand all that comes against it."

"That is true. But if we love each other, which we do, that love will endure. I love you too much to wreck our chance for a lifetime of happiness. Remember what I told you at the conference in Chicago. I told you I wanted our marriage to honor God. Well, in order for me to be the right kind of husband and a good father to our children, I first need to resolve these issues before me. Only then will I feel confident going into a marriage.

"Jane, I don't want my love for you to be a sacrifice to this craziness. If I were to lose you plus my lawsuit, I don't know if I could continue to fight the battle any longer."

"You're not going to lose me, Michael. I'm here. What does that tell you?"

Michael smiled.

"Former white supremacist Donald Sykes," announced the news anchor, "has made official his plans to run for governor."

"I feel I will overcome my second-place finish in last fall's U.S. Senate race," Sykes told the reporter, a white man. "That's because Louisiana voters now recognize my policy positions as mainstream."

The reporter concluded. "Sykes received 65 percent of the state's white vote in last year's bid for the U.S. Senate seat."

"Well, he's up to it again," said Michael. "Why did I ever move to this Godforsaken place?"

"Because they offered you a lot of money and a prestigious job," answered Jane.

"Yes," said Michael. "But, how was I to know that it came at such a high price?"

In September 1989, Michael began his third and final year at the Institute. His career was on the verge of ruin.

People at the Institute had stopped talking to him. Even Doris avoided him. But Michael wanted to confront the liberal Doris. He felt that if any of the power players opened up to him, it would be Doris. Not wanting others to witness his conversation with her, he simply showed up at her house one night around nine-thirty.

He knocked on the door but there was no answer. He heard voices so he opened the door and walked inside. He saw clothes lying on the floor, making a trail to Doris' bedroom. From the bedroom he could hear Doris crying out in a louder and louder voice to the point where she almost screamed - "Fuck me! Fuck me! Fuck me! Nig-ger!!!"

Michael rushed out of the house and ran to his car. As he fumbled for the ignition, he broke down and cried. "Tyrone! Oh God! What's happened?"

Michael had to continue his work even though he was depressed and angry. The next evening, he taught his graduate seminar in public policy implementation. One of the main topics was equal opportunity and affirmative action. This was a hot topic not only because of his employment situation, which most of the students were aware of, but also because of the popularity of Donald Sykes, who represented white backlash against affirmative action.

Michael wanted the students to clearly understand affirmative action and not confuse it with racial quotas as many right-wing politicians wanted them to. He started the discussion off by setting up a scenario. He said: "Suppose there is going to be a race one year from now between Nate and Wilfred. Let us say that Wilfred has the freedom to prepare as he pleases. On the other hand, Nate's movement is restricted by those who will sponsor the race. Nate is also provided a mediocre diet. After one year Nate is given his freedom. In words, the 1964 Civil Rights Act is passed. Now, Nate is expected to compete equally with Wilfred. Can he? No, he cannot. However, is Nate's inability to compete equally with Wilfred based upon Nate's genetic inferiority or is it the result of preferential treatment given to Wilfred at Nate's expense?

"The question is, should a government which sanctioned discriminatory laws, robbing Nate of his constitutional rights to fair treatment, take an affirmative stance to correct those past injustices by helping Nate to overcome them?"

Most of the students seemed to understand the point Michael was trying to make, but they remained committed to the beliefs they had probably grown up with. All Michael could do was challenge them to think.

"Unfortunately," Michael said, "Too often we as Americans tend to think that any Black or Hispanic who receives a job is unqualified but gets the job anyway because of affirmative action. As long as this mentality pervades the workplace, the public and private sectors will both continue to suffer, and we as a nation will never realize our true potential. America's people are her greatest asset. A divided America will never maximize her total potential either in world politics or in the marketplace."

Michael paused. He looked out across the classroom, above the heads of the students, as if searching for the right words. Then, he continued. "Affirmative action is a policy that encourages organizations to aggressively recruit qualified minorities and women in order to fill diversity goals. It does not exclude any group from competing fairly for the job or the admissions process. Quotas, on the other hand, do prevent non-targeted groups from being considered. That is why the U.S. Supreme Court has outlawed quotas as a form of reverse discrimination."

The next morning, on his way to the Institute building, Michael was met by Gracie Mullen, as he entered the building's stairwell. Gracie was out of breath. She seemed to have run down the three flights of stairs to meet him.

"Here," said Gracie. She handed him a flier. "You should come to this anti-Sykes rally on Saturday."

She rushed back up the stairs ahead of him. Michael sensed that Gracie did not want to be seen soliciting protesters for the rally.

When Michael got home that evening, he telephoned his neighbors, Scott and Beth Harper and told them about the rally. He also called Freddie and Kirk from his church. The Harpers agreed to go. So did Freddie and Kirk.

This was the first time Michael had ever been a part of any political rally. He made up his own hand-held sign that Saturday morning. It read, "No Fascist Governor." It had a swastika drawn at its center. Scott and Beth made signs that read, "No Racist Governor." Freddie, Kirk, Constance, and Susie all showed up just as Michael and Scott were finishing up their signs.

As soon as Freddie and his friends finished making signs that read "No KKK Governor" and "No Nazi Governor," the two groups left. As they approached City Park, they found a sea of cars lining Wisner Boulevard and Carrollton Avenue near the New Orleans Museum of Art where the march would start.

The march was led by people Michael identified as left-wing extremists. They shouted from their hand-held loudspeakers, "Say No to Sykes! Say No to Reagan! Say No to Racism!" A sea of hand-held signs read, "No Sykes!" Many of the cars displayed "No Sykes!" bumper stickers.

It seemed to Michael as if individuals with nothing else in common had joined against a common enemy. Michael knew that President Reagan had publicly opposed the campaign of Donald Sykes and had refused to acknowledge Sykes as a fellow Republican, but, that did not seem to matter to the protest march leaders. They categorized all conservatives as part of Sykes' right wing extremist fringe.

Periodically, the shouts of the marchers would be drowned out by Sykes supporters who had strategically positioned themselves along the parade route. From the sidewalks they shouted to the top of their lungs, "Sykes! Sykes! Sykes! Sykes! Sykes! Sykes! Sykes!"

Michael saw one group of about twenty Sykes followers who were apparently college fraternity boys. They were dressed in starched khakis and button-down collar shirts, their fraternity pins shining in the mid-morning sun. One of them caught Michael staring at his group. As he looked back at Michael, Michael could feel evil radiating from his blue eyes.

The protesters marched down Esplanade Avenue to Rampart Street, where the march ended at Louis Armstrong Park. There, it turned into a full political rally. Now the speakers were state and local political leaders. There were white Republican conservatives and moderate Democrats who opposed Sykes. There were leftists like those who had led the protest march. And there were liberals like Mitch Deveaux. "Sykes and his messengers of hate," Deveaux preached to the cheering crowd, "will be defeated again and again until the truth is revealed."

Michael saw Tyrone Lockett in the crowd. The two had not seen each other in months. "Excuse me," Michael said to Scott, Beth and the others, "I see someone I need to say hello to."

"Good to see you here," said Tyrone, as he looked up and saw Michael walking in his direction, and as they greeted each other warmly.

"Glad you're here too," said Michael. Adding, "I'm just impressed that so many people turned out for the rally, and feel strongly enough about Sykes to make a statement like this against him."

"There must be at least a thousand people here," said Tyrone. "It's good they're from different races and religions."

"How are things going with you and Doris?" Michael asked.

"Very rocky," Tyrone replied. "But she did tell me about what happened to you at the Institute. I'm sorry to hear about that."

"Well brother," responded Michael, "unfortunately, that's the world we live in. So, when is the last time you saw Doris?"

"It's been at least a month," replied Tyrone.

If that was the case, Michael realized that it could not have been Tyrone with Doris the night he stopped by her house.

"Is she seeing anyone else?" he asked.

"Not that I know of," said Tyrone. "But, you know, she always has some black or Latin dude on call."

"Hey," said Michael. "Let's get together for dinner next week and talk some more."

"Sure," said Tyrone.

"Monday, seven o'clock, at my house, is that okay?"

"I'll be there."

Monday at dinner, Michael told Tyrone what he had heard the night he stopped by Doris' house.

"I'm not surprised. She tried that stuff with me. That's why we're not together anymore," responded Tyrone.

"That's probably very smart of you," Michael replied.

"No matter how much I tried to make things work with Doris, I always felt she was using me," Tyrone explained. "It's like I was never good enough for her. It's like she was just using me for sex. Other than that, I was a nobody. You know, I believe there is something sinister about Doris but I don't know what.

Tyrone continued to think aloud. "I just cannot understand her obsession with these white supremacy groups. And something else, in spite of all of her liberalism, she does not have one black female friend. That is, if you exclude professional acquaintances."

"You know, you're right," agreed Michael. "I was totally in Doris' corner until I heard her at her house that night. That, plus her shunning me at the Institute, has opened my eyes." Michael paused. He had an idea but hesitated to speak it.

"What are you thinking?" asked Tyrone.

"What if you pretend to want her back," Michael began slowly. "But use it to try to find out more about her. And you might also find out what happened to me."

"I might be able to do that," responded Tyrone.

"Seriously," said Michael. "Doris might know something about whether or not Bernstein was actually treated fairly. She might even know something about the black professor who was fired seven years ago, before they hired me."

"I will do it," said Tyrone. "But not just for you. I want to find out more about her for my own peace of mind."

Tyrone called Doris on the telephone later that night and asked if they could try their relationship again. "I knew you'd come crawling back to me," she told him.

"When can I see you?" Tyrone asked.

"What's wrong with tomorrow night?" Doris replied. "Be here at eight o'clock."

When he got home from work the next day, Tyrone found a message from Doris on his answering machine. "This is Doris. I may be running a little late this evening so just in case, I've left the key in its usual place. Make yourself at home."

Tyrone arrived at her house right after six o'clock. He had never gone through Doris' personal belongings before. Now, it was a different story. He wanted to find out as much about her as possible.

He searched the closets, dresser drawers, file cabinets and everywhere else he could think of. After about 45 minutes he decided to open a cedar chest. Inside he found a locked letter box. He broke it open. Inside he found a letter from the *Committee to Elect Donald Sykes Governor* that thanked Doris for her financial support through the current campaign. Another letter made reference to the Institute of Public Policy and commended Doris and other members of the Institute for their role in bringing the policy concerns of America's silent majority to the political mainstream.

At that moment Doris walked in. "What do you think you are doing?" she demanded.

"Can you explain this?" Tyrone shouted. "Can you tell me who else at the Institute is supporting this racist?"

Doris walked over to Tyrone and jerked the letters from his hand. "Don't tell me you are surprised. You know you were nothing to me but my pleasure toy."

Then, with a condescending stare, she added, "It's not like you didn't get anything in return. Let's have a drink."

As Doris turned and walked towards the kitchen, Tyrone realized his attraction to and desire for her were still alive. It was the way she intentionally walked in that tight skirt that brought back memories and made him lose his way.

"Can I make love to her and yet not trust her?" he asked himself. "Can I make love to a known enemy?"

Doris came out of the kitchen completely naked with a bottle of scotch, two glasses and a bucket of ice. Tyrone immediately began to rip off his clothes. Doris walked into her bedroom, poured the drinks, and waited for him on the settee. As Tyrone walked into the bedroom, Doris began her drink and handed him his. He drank it in one swallow.

She stood up and pulled him to her so that they were in complete body contact. "One more time for old time's sake?" Doris asked.

"Yes!" responded Tyrone. He picked her up, placed her on the bed, and began to make love to her.

Doris began to murmur obscenities and use racially derogatory language. As Tyrone entered her, a sharp knife pierced his side. As he rolled over, he was pierced again in the abdomen, and again in the chest, the stomach, the face.

"Congratulations! You have become more than my pleasure servant. You have become a security risk," were Doris' last words to her black lover.

Before taking a shower and getting dressed, Doris lit a cigarette and dialed the telephone.

"I have had to fix a security leak and it was messy. I need Rogers down here right away."

A couple of hours later two men showed up at Doris' door carrying a suitcase. "He's in the bedroom," she told them. She lit another cigarette as she pointed the way.

Rogers shook his head when saw the body. "Well, the good thing is, now there's one less nigger in the world. But you don't have to fuck'em to kill'em," he said to her.

A shaken but determined Doris glared at Rogers. "Don't preach to me dammit!"

Rogers clenched his fists and began to approach Doris. But the stronger and more muscular Beau grabbed him from behind and held him back. "No. Let's take of our business, man." Rogers rolled his eyes at Doris and turned away. He opened the suitcase and took out a black body bag. Rogers and Beau put Tyrone's naked body in the bag and wrapped it in a floor rug from Doris dining room. They carried the bundle out to a van and drove off.

As soon as they left, Doris began to go through Tyrone's clothes. She found his keys in his pants pocket. Putting his clothes in the suitcase the men had left behind, she drove Tyrone's car to his apartment and placed his clothes alongside his bed and his keys on the nightstand. It was three o'clock in the morning. She was picked up several blocks away from the apartment building by the men in the van.

In the weeks that followed, Michael called Tyrone several evenings but got no answer. He decided to try him at work. "Tyrone is not the type of person to just disappear without telling anyone," Tyrone's supervisor at the community college told Michael.

"I agree," said Michael. "The police should be contacted. I have a feeling that something terrible has happened to him."

"What?" asked the supervisor.

"I don't know. I just have a feeling."

The police were contacted by the community college at the urging of Tyrone's supervisor. The supervisor told police to talk to Michael Woods.

The policemen came to Michael's house that afternoon. "I suggest you check with Doris Neuhaus, Tyrone's ex-girlfriend," Michael told them. "Tyrone said he was getting back together with her. He was excited. It all happened around the same time he disappeared. As a matter of fact, it was the same week that he disappeared."

The two police officers, a white man and a black man, went to Doris' house later that evening after a fruitless search of Tyrone's apartment. When they pushed the play button on Tyrone's answering machine, they found only Michael's messages.

The police officers knocked on Doris' door around seven o'clock. "May we come in?" said the white officer. "We have some questions to ask you about the disappearance of an acquaintance of yours - a Mr. Tyrone Lockett."

"Sure, come in," said Doris. "I heard that he was missing. Please have a seat. Can I get you something?"

"No ma'am. Hopefully, this won't take long," responded the white officer.

The two officers seated themselves on Doris white leather sofa. Doris sat in the matching chair across from them. "Can you tell us when was the last time you saw or spoke to Mr. Lockett?" asked the black officer.

"Unfortunately, I broke up with him a couple of months ago and I haven't seen him since."

"Didn't he try to contact you recently?" asked the officer.

"As a matter of fact, he did call me," Doris responded. "But I told him I never wanted to see him again. I do wish that I could be of some help but I don't know anything. I'm sorry that he's disappeared. I, I just hope it's not because I blew him off."

"Well, thank you ma'am," said the white officer, "We're just checking all possible leads in the hope that something will pay off. Please let us know if you do hear from him."

"No problem," replied Doris, as she and the officers stood up and headed for the door. "And, will you please let me know if you hear something. I'd like to know that he's okay."

"Maybe he's just love sick," said the black officer as he smirked at Doris. "Maybe he'll eventually show up on his own." Doris' big, green eyes flashed her appreciation for the officer's flattery.

Michael called the police station from work later that week and asked for an update on the investigation. He spoke to the white officer working the case.

"We still have no hard leads," said the officer. "He's not home but his car keys and belongings are there. That's all we know. Maybe he'll turn up on his own."

Frustrated, Michael decided to query Doris himself. He walked down the hall and tapped on her door.

"Oh, come in," said Doris, swiveling her chair around. "Have a seat."

"That's okay," said Michael. "I'll stand."

"What can I do for you?" asked Doris.

"Well, I guess you know that there is a missing person's report filed on Tyrone."

"Yes. I know. Some police officers came by my house this week asking about him. As I told them, I don't know anything. I don't know if you know this or not but we were no longer seeing each other."

"He told me the two of you had gotten back together."

"He must have been mistaken," explained Doris. "He did call me but I told him I never wanted to see him again. That's what I told the police. But I do hope that he's all right."

Michael looked at Doris. Her face radiated sincerity. He sensed that she was hiding something behind that perfect smile. He just didn't know what.

Chapter Six

It was more than simply another workday. It was a workday in February 1990, Michael's final semester at the Institute. Michael walked into the main office and checked his mailbox at 3 p.m., right before going home. He had finished with his classes for the day and he had no more appointments.

In his box was a letter from *American Journal of Public Policy*. A rush of inner emotion moved through Michael's body. "So, this is the final rejection letter," he thought to himself. Michael nonchalantly put the envelope in his trench coat pocket. He didn't think he could stand any more bad news right now. He wanted to just throw the letter away without opening it. "Why put myself through more misery?" he asked.

Michael spent the rest of the afternoon at his home office preparing job applications and surveying the job announcements in the *Public Policy Newsletter*. After an hour or so, he had psychologically cushioned himself for whatever information the letter from *AJPP* contained. So, he carelessly opened the envelope, totally prepared for the rejection.

"Congratulations," the letter stated, "The manuscript you submitted on 'Privatization and the impact of local political culture,' has been accepted for publication in the *American Journal of Public Policy*."

This news was bitter sweet. Michael could have made more sense out of his life if it had been a rejection letter. Now, how could he explain Barney Holtz's insistence that the manuscript was useless? The letter meant that Michael had met the Institute's requirement for refereed journal publications, including at least one in a major journal.

He had succeeded. And yet he had failed because no one at the Institute cared.

The telephone on his desk rang. It was Orville, a senior colleague from the Institute. "I have some information that may be helpful to you. Can you meet me in one hour behind the museum at City Park?"

"Sure, but what's it about?"

"I can't talk now. Will you come?"

"Okay. I'll be there."

Michael understood that most people at the Institute did not want to be seen talking to him because of his lawsuit. The Institute could retaliate against people who seemed to be in his corner. But Orville was near retirement. He had nothing to fear from the Institute. Michael was curious. As he left the house, Michael checked his caller ID and discovered that Orville had even called him from a pay telephone.

Dusk was falling as Michael drove up the long tree lined driveway to the museum. He saw Orville in the distance waving at him. Michael pulled up toward the back of the building, and Orville got into the car.

"So, what's so important that you have to meet me in secret?" asked Michael. "I'm dying to know."

"Well," said Orville, "Some of us, including John Walker, have uncovered some damaging information on certain people at the Institute."

"What is it? What information?"

"We are only now at the point where we may be able to substantiate parts of it but John and I want to cautiously alert you of the potential bombshell." Orville paused as if he were carefully selecting his words. "If what we suspect is true, your troubles at the Institute run deeper than you think. There is an ongoing program to systematically discredit nonwhites and Jews."

"What do you mean? What are you talking about?" Michael asked.

"We have evidence," explained Orville, "that Barry Bonds is a member of SWAN, the highly secretive Society of White Aryan Nation."

"Is that the same Aryan Nation group up in Hayden Lake, Idaho?" asked Michael.

"No," said Orville. "This group's wealth and sophistication make Aryan Nation look like the Beverly Hillbillies. What I mean is, at least, before Granny and Jed got their money."

"I've never heard of them," responded Michael.

"Not many people have. It's that secretive."

Orville sensed tension building within Michael. His anger was starting to show.

"You must control yourself," counseled Orville. "I know this is difficult for you to stomach. But you must use your head and not your emotions!"

As Orville talked, Michael realized that he had found someone who cared about the truth. Like Michael, Orville cared enough about the truth to value it over all other things.

"John has been collaborating with one of his former students who is an FBI investigator," said Orville. "Through their efforts, they have verified regular correspondence between Bonds and SWAN members from across the country."

"I wonder if Bonds' offer to coauthor the conference paper with me was arranged solely to discredit me as incompetent," Michael pondered aloud.

"I'm not a betting man," responded Orville. "But, if I were, I'd put my money on it."

"And all this time," Michael said, "I've been thinking that Bonds was a homosexual and stopped working on the research project with me because I ridiculed him."

"Whether he is or whether he is not is beside the point. If you had responded positively to his advances, you would just have given them one more round of ammunition to use against you."

Tears filled Michael's eyes.

"Regardless," said Orville, "we suspect that Bonds is not the only one involved. There is no telling how high up this will go."

"Did Bernstein know about this?" inquired Michael, as he wiped his eyes dry.

"He suspected it," said Orville. "As soon as he said anything, he was found dead in his bath tub in Covington. His wife found him. That's pretty sad, you know. He was shot in the head. His neighbors say they heard nothing."

"How well did the police investigate?"

"The Covington police insist they did a proper investigation. But, upon being given evidence of Bernstein's diagnosed depression, they ruled his death a suicide."

"Why didn't you and John say something to them?"

"There was no way we could have proved anything back then," explained Orville. "If we had opened our mouths everything would have blown up in our faces."

Orville paused again and looked hard at Michael. "Before I go, I want to tell you to be careful who you share this information with. Your personal safety and that of others will depend upon it."

"I understand."

"Well," said Orville, "John and I just felt it was about time you knew."

"Thank you," said Michael.

Orville got out of the car and walked towards the park. Michael went back to his house and sat at the desk in his home study. He picked up the telephone to call Jane and put it back down. He was too worked up to talk. He would write her a letter instead. That way, she'd have evidence of his top-secret conversation with Orville. He wrote:

> "...what better way to destroy a race than to have that
> race buy into the notion that it is inferior. If I
> believe that I am incapable of meeting the standards
> of the Institute then I have accepted the fact
> that regardless of my attending the best schools,
> and adopting the right attitude and behavior, I am
> still only a nigger and that explains my failure.
>
> Thus, I would have to believe that I can never over-
> come my innate incompetence derived from my
> inferior racial heritage. If this is the case,
> one may rightfully conclude that the white liberal

establishment has done its best through affirmative action and other liberal policies to help bring a lower level of being to a point where he was never meant to be. As a result, society would be justified in a denial of racial equality in the workplace based upon the inability of highly trained blacks to perform at the same level as similarly trained whites."

Several days later the Institute circulated a memorandum. Michael got a copy of it from his office mailbox. "Institute of Public Policy Director Mitzie Schultz," the memo stated, "will be a featured speaker at the nationally televised forum on the 'Donald Sykes phenomenon, right-wing politics, and the future of civil rights policy.' The forum will be held at the Louisiana Superdome on February 19, 1990 at 7:00 P.M."

Michael went to the forum alone. He wanted to hear what Mitzie had to say. Michael pondered several questions in his head as he drove his car down Poydras Street to the Superdome entrance. Could Mitzie be a member of this white supremacist group Orville had talked about? If so, who else was a member? Was Matt Kohl a member? Was Barney Holtz? Did that explain Barney's insistence that his manuscript was useless?

Mitzie, along with Barbara Potts of the Southern Christian Leadership Conference, was introduced to the audience as a proponent of aggressive civil rights and affirmative action policies. Also on the panel was Dr. William Harrison of the National Enterprise Institute, a conservative think-tank. Other moderates and conservatives were also introduced.

"I am a supporter," Mitzie said, "of race-based policies in the workplace. However, there is a cogent reason as to why I am a supporter of such policies. The reason is Affirmative Action. Affirmative Action is the only method we have to ensure that racial minorities, who have been discriminated against in the past, get their chance at the American dream. To deny them that opportunity is un-American."

"I take strong issue with that statement!" declared Dr. Harrison. "Who are you to say what's American and what's un-American?"

The audience mumbled.

"It is characters such this and other right-wing conservatives," Mitzie countered, "who feed on the fears of whites. They tell whites that African Americans are taking away their livelihoods. It is not true. Yet these fears comprise the heart of the Donald Sykes phenomenon."

Mitzie held up a booklet. "This study, conducted by the polling unit at the Institute for Public Policy, substantiates my position. It provides statistical evidence that white men maintain and control the great majority of management, corporate and government positions in America. Furthermore, it shows how the trend is increasing once the variable white women is controlled for."

Mitzie placed the booklet back on the table. "Finally," she said, conservative political rhetoric claims that careers of whites are being ruined by affirmative action. Well, our study shows that the percentage of whites whose careers are negatively impacted by affirmative action is so small as to be insignificant. In conclusion, may I say that African Americans are no threat. They only want their opportunity to achieve the American dream."

Harrison responded. "Conservatives support equal treatment in the workplace and elsewhere. Some moderate conservatives even support affirmative action policies. However, we believe that it is not enough to have this type of policy if it is not being administered in fairness to all groups regardless of race. Reverse discrimination is just as wrong."

Dr. Harrison picked up his booklet and briefly held it up. "Our studies suggest a need for a national review of such policies to investigate their true effectiveness as well as their impact on the American psyche. If our preliminary studies are correct, perhaps an economic based affirmative action plan would be healthier psychologically. If that's not possible, indicators show that it would be best to scrap the policy altogether."

Dr. Harrison paused. He turned and stared sarcastically at Mitzie. "And, may I say one last thing for the benefit of Dr. Schultz only. Please do not paint us all with your broad brush."

Attorney Gloria Potts of the Southern Christian Leadership Conference responded to Dr. Harrison's comments. "As a black American, I am too much aware of the subtle forms of racism that continue to pervade every nook and cranny of American society. The American workplace is no exception.

"To scrap affirmative action simply because it may inconvenience some whites is a slap in the face to all Americans of African heritage who believe in America. It is telling them that despite lofty ideals, America does not care that they were denied equality for hundreds of years. It is telling them that America does not care to guarantee that their futures will be protected from subtle and overt forms of racism because the White American is, and always will be, and always has been, of greater value."

The last speakers were two white men who straddled the fence on affirmative action. They seemed to hate both affirmative action and Donald Sykes. Their hatred for Donald Sykes made them lean more towards a lukewarm version of affirmative action which from Michael's perspective was quite similar to Dr. Harrison's conservative position.

After the forum, a reception was held for invited guests only. Michael had received no invitation. As he walked toward the exit, he could feel the camaraderie and mutual sense of purpose that seemed to define conversations among Mitzie, Gloria Potts, and other liberals as they escorted one another toward the reception hall.

Michael left the Superdome wanting desperately to believe that Mitzie's words were sincere. But he knew a different Mitzie, a Mitzie too eager to believe negative rumors that might destroy everything he had worked for.

When Mitzie Schultz left the Superdome, she took a taxi to the Saint Charles Inn. She unlocked a door with a key she took from her purse. "I'm here. How did you enjoy the forum?" she asked.

"It was perfect," said Mickey Calabrese, lying on the bed, shirtless. "It was just as perfect as you are. I almost died waiting for you. Come here!"

That Monday morning, Michael walked across the campus from the library on his way to the Institute. He ran into Erroll Fontenot.

"How are you holding up?" Erroll asked.

"I'm doing fine, I guess. Anything new in the grapevine?"

"Well, the word is that your director is lobbying the provost to double the salary of your current line so they can recruit at the full professor level."

"Why are they doing that?"

"Well, she claims that although the Institute is committed to racial diversity, they can't afford to gamble on another unproven black Ph.D. If they have to hire another black, according to them, it has to be someone who is already established."

Erroll looked at him sympathetically. "You hang in there now. I'm sure you're going to land on your feet."

"Thanks, Erroll," said Michael. The plan, according to a memo which Michael took from his office mailbox that Tuesday, was

> "...to make it clear to the administration that the Institute is doing everything in its power to diversify its faculty but refuses to sacrifice quality and the Institute's professional reputation in the process. Thus, we need to recruit at the full professor level and we need the necessary funding from the university in order to proceed."

The memo was written by Elliott Nussmeyer, whom Mitzie had appointed as head of the search committee responsible for finding Michael's replacement.

As Michael was reading the memo in his office with the door closed, he heard a knock. He got up and opened the door. Gracie Mullen quietly walked into Michael's office and closed the door behind her.

"You don't mind if I close the door, do you? There is something important I need to talk to you about."

"I don't mind," said Michael, as he sat back down at his desk. "What is it?"

"Well, I thought you should know about a conversation I overheard taking place between Nussmeyer and Tullock. They were talking in the copy room. The machines were running and the copy room door was almost closed but I could still hear."

"What did they say?"

"Nussmeyer told Tullock that the Institute should never hire an established black scholar because of the high salary they demand. Tullock then said that Mitzie had assured him that the provost would never fork over the money anyway. So, they didn't have to worry about anything."

Gracie put her hands on her face to help compose herself. "I can't believe what Nussmeyer said next."

"What did he say?"

"He said that senior faculty here should not have to put up with the nightmare of having one of those sambo props making more money than them. And you know what? Tullock agreed with him. This is so disgusting. These people make me ashamed to be white. We're not all like that, Dr. Woods."

"I know, Gracie. I know. Here. Have a seat."

Michael pulled a chair from the wall and closer to his desk. Gracie sat in the chair and remained quiet. Michael's heart was pounding faster than Gracie's. He was remembering what Orville had said to him at City Park.

"Is that all they said?" asked Michael.

"No," said Gracie as she put her hands to her face again.

"They said that they needed to convince the administration that the Institute is committed to the highest standards and refuses to sacrifice it for diversity. They said they would hold to that position until Calabrese's office leaves them alone.'"

"So, you're saying that they don't want to hire any black professors and are only using the high standards argument as a smoke screen?"

"That's exactly what I heard them say," said Gracie. "It's all so unfair, though. They see no problem hiring unproven white Ph.Ds. Look at Mark Vandenberg. He hasn't published one thing since he's been here. And Dr. Neuhaus' publication record was the same as yours in her third year." "I agree, Gracie," said Michael. "I agree."

Michael thought for several seconds as Gracie looked at him with sympathy. "Well, I guess there's nothing that can be done about it internally. I've already lost my grievance and my job. Would you be willing to tell the court what you heard?"

"I don't know. I really can't afford to get involved in your lawsuit. I need my job. There's no telling what these people here would do to me. I only told you because you need to know. Maybe it will allow you to feel better about yourself."

"I understand," said Michael.

"Dr. Woods, if push comes to shove maybe I'll have another job by then and I can do it. It's just that I can't say yes right now. Do you understand?"

"Yes. I understand."

A solemn Gracie got up from the chair and cautiously opened Michael's office door. "Look and see if anyone is in the hallway" she whispered to Michael.

Michael got up and looked out the door. "The coast is clear."

On March 5, while walking through the student union building, Michael picked up a copy of the student newspaper, *The Reveler*. He had just bought an ice cream cone at the grill when the front-page story caught his attention. The headline read: "Williams a Finalist for Hawaii Post."

Michael read the story as he walked across the campus and back to his office. Hodge Williams had been named a finalist for president of the University of Hawaii. The writer of the story interviewed Provost Mickey Calabrese and asked him to speculate on who the next Orleans president might be if Williams left.

"There has been pressure for some time now," Calabrese was quoted as saying, "that it is time for Orleans to have a woman president. That is, if one is found who is qualified and capable."

The reporter quoted Calabrese as saying that the pressure to hire a woman came from alumni but "it does not exclude a man from getting the job. However, if a woman is found who is equally qualified, the preference will be given to her. The University's commitment to affirmative action would be unquestioned with a woman at the helm."

Chapter Seven

On March 15, John Walker received a telephone call at home from an acquaintance involved in the secret investigation of the Institute. The man told John that former student and FBI agent Maurice Broussard would contact him soon to arrange a face-to-face meeting.

John, having been sure for the past month that he was onto something big, could not wait. He immediately telephoned Broussard. "What have you found?" he asked.

"You shouldn't have called," said Maurice. "I can't talk to you over the phone."

"That bad, huh?"

"Yeah, it is. Hey, since we're already talking, can you come to Washington next week during your Spring Break?"

"Wouldn't it be easier just to see you the next time you're in New Orleans? You're always down here."

"That's not a good idea. We really shouldn't be talking now," said Broussard. "Don't call anymore. Let me contact you. Good-bye."

The conversation troubled John. He knew Broussard enough to know that Broussard was frightened.

"This crazy investigation," John said to himself, "has gotten bigger than I ever expected it to get." John knew he was just a disgruntled professor wanting revenge against the powers that be. Now it appeared that his quest might endanger the lives of his friends as well as threaten his own safety.

John was a political conservative. He had been one all of his life, but he had never considered himself a racist. That label had been bestowed upon him by individuals with whom he blatantly disagreed about on certain areas of public policy.

But now, having been labeled a racist, sexist, and bigot for so long, John was no longer sure what he was. He was certain only that encouraging Broussard to investigate the Institute might reveal the truth and turn the tables on his colleagues. The following evening John received an anonymous email, informing him of the time and place to meet.

On Wednesday of the third week in March, during the middle of Spring Break, a solemn John Walker took a 7:30 a.m. flight to Washington National Airport. He was prepared to spend a few extra days in Washington in case the situation demanded it.

His meeting with Broussard was scheduled for noon, at the corner of 17th and Flint, an area plagued with crack houses and poverty. At 11:45 a.m., John stepped off the subway train. He glanced at his watch. He walked swiftly in the direction of 17th Street. As he came up the hill, he could see Maurice standing beside a rundown house. Maurice was talking to a bearded, middle-aged man. John assumed the man was a fellow agent working on the investigation.

As John crossed the street to the block where Maurice and the man were standing, Maurice looked up and made eye contact. At that moment gunfire erupted from out of nowhere. Maurice and the stranger were both hit. As they fell to the ground, John could see the side of Maurice's face being blown away.

John looked up and saw the trigger man on the third floor of the rundown building. The trigger man fired at John and missed. John ran into a vacant building and out the back, through a back alley covered with gang graffiti.

Two men got out of a slow-moving vehicle and chased John until they lost him in the back alley where he hid in an abandoned garage. But they had seen him. They could tell their higher ups the second man killed was not John Walker but a stranger who had stopped to talk to Broussard. The driver stopped to make a phone call. "A mistake has been made. The bird is still flying. But it's only a matter of time before we cage it."

"Do it ASAP!" came the reply. "Do it before he flies south again."

The two men, Mike Rogers and Beau Lapiere, returned to FBI headquarters where they informed their superiors that the New Orleans investigation was winding down to one dangerous right-wing extremist named John Walker. They reported that agent Broussard's top-secret meeting with Walker had turned out to be an ambush.

The bureau issued an all-points bulletin for John Walker and placed him on the agency's "Ten Most Wanted List." FBI agents were placed at major airports, train stations, and bus stations. The official manhunt bulletin described Walker as "a white supremacist wanted for killing an FBI agent investigating right wing hate groups." The bulletin said Walker should be considered "armed and dangerous."

John decided he should stay in the abandoned garage. He spent the night there. At daybreak John left the building and searched for a pay phone. He saw one as he neared the downtown area. Adjacent to the pay phone was a newspaper stand. On the front page was a story with his picture under the caption: "White Supremacist Sought in Slaying of FBI Agent."

John took the calling card from his wallet and immediately telephoned Orville. The answering machine came on. He hung up and dialed Orville's office number. There was no answer.

"Shit!" John said. He then dialed Alex Sanchez. A woman answered the phone.

"Hello, Marguerite! This is John Walker. Is Alex there?"

"Oh John!" the wife said. "Alex is dead. He was killed in an automobile crash on his way home last night."

"Oh no!" John responded. "Marguerite, I have something very important to say. You have to be able to take this. There is a good possibility that Alex was murdered by the same people who killed Maurice and attempted to kill me yesterday."

"Maurice is dead?" she asked.

"Yes," John replied. "He was killed here in D.C. right before my eyes. It was horrible. But even worse, I have been framed for the murder of one of my best friends."

"What is going on?" Marguerite demanded.

"For your own safety it's best I not go into details," John replied. "But please, do not believe what you read about me."

Before hanging up John said, "Please try to relay to Orville Reid what I just told you. Every time I call him, I get an answering machine. And, I don't want to leave any detailed messages. Tell him. He will understand. Goodbye Marguerite"

John then started to call his wife Kathy. He then stopped. He realized Kathy was unaware of the Institute's activities and it was perhaps best that she not know. On the other hand, he did not want her to believe what she would read in the newspaper. So, he called. The answering machine came on.

"Hello Kathy! This is John. I cannot explain anything to you now. I just want to say that I am innocent and I love you."

John then called Orville's home number once more. The answering machine picked up again. This time John decided to leave a very brief message. "Orville. This is John Walker. I'm in Washington. I had a meeting with Maurice yesterday. He was shot and killed and I've been framed. I thought you should know. Please, keep yourself safe."

Orville and Mrs. Reid came home that Thursday evening after spending two days with their son and his family in Biloxi. "Oh, it was so nice having two whole days in Biloxi with the grandchildren," said Mrs. Reid, as she entered the house and began unloading a bag of souvenirs. "Kaitlin is just getting bigger and bigger. Before long she'll be as big as her brother Josh."

"Yeah, they get bigger and bigger," said Orville, as he placed the luggage bags beside the sofa and headed toward the restroom.

"Oh! We have some messages," said Ms. Reid, as she looked at the answering machine on the end table. She walked over to the table with the plastic bag still in her hand and pushed the play button. "Orville. This is John Walker. I'm in Washington. I had a meeting with Maurice yesterday. He was shot and killed and I've been framed. I thought you should know. Please, keep yourself safe."

Mrs. Reid dropped the bag of porcelain souvenirs to the floor. Orville, still in the restroom, heard the porcelain objects break. "Is everything okay?" he asks, as he opened the bathroom door and came out.

Mrs. Reid was standing above the bag of broken porcelain, looking as if she had seen a ghost. Orville rushed over to her. "What is it? Is it your heart again? Sit down. Relax. Take some deep breaths. I'm calling the ambulance."

"No!" shouted Mrs. Reid. "It's not my heart. It's that answering machine. It's that message on the answering machine."

Orville pushed the play button. "Orville. This is John Walker. I'm in Washington. I had a meeting with Broussard yesterday. He was shot and killed and I've been framed. I thought you should know. Please, keep yourself safe."

"What is this?" demanded Mrs. Reid, as she turned and looked at Orville.

"It involves the FBI and some investigations into white supremacy groups. John and Maurice were working on it," said Orville, as he sat down in the chair across from the sofa. "That's all I can say. If I say any more, your own safety may be at risk. You understand?"

"Yes," said Mrs. Reid, as she sat down on the sofa. "Yes."

Yet, Mrs. Reid remained alarmed all night and into the next day when she pleaded with Orville not to leave the house to buy groceries. "Please, don't go. I'm so afraid. We can have our groceries delivered to the house here. I've done it before. Just let me call the supermarket."

She went into the kitchen to get the number. She then brought it back to the living room where Orville sat and began to dial the number.

"Please hang up the phone for a minute," said Orville. "Let's talk about this first." Mrs. Reid, sitting on the sofa next to her husband, placed the receiver on the end table.

"Perhaps it would be best if I keep my regular routine," explained Orville. "I have no idea if these supremacists even know John has informed me of the FBI investigation. If they are watching me, I must not give them any reason to be suspicious."

The telephone rang. Mrs. Reid picked it up. "It's for you Orville." She gave the receiver to her husband.

"Hello."

"Professor Reid?"

"Yes."

"This is Marguerite. Alex was killed in an accident on his way home from Baton Rouge."

"Oh! I'm sorry to hear that Marguerite. I am truly sorry. Is there anything we can do?"

"Oh God! I'm so afraid!" exclaimed Marguerite. "John Walker called yesterday morning. He's being sought for the murder of Maurice - but says he was framed by the actual killer. He said the same people may have killed my husband. My God! What do you know about this?"

"I don't know much of anything. The best we can all do is just stay calm until this thing is taken care of. There is nothing else to do, Marguerite."

"He told me to tell you and you'd understand. What does he mean by that?"

"I'm sorry Marguerite. I've told you all I know. Let's hope that Alex's death is not connected with what happened in Washington. Okay? It may not be connected at all."

"Goodbye Professor Reid."

"Goodbye Marguerite."

"What was that all about," asked Mrs. Reid? Someone else is dead?"

"John Walker called Marguerite too. He was trying to reach Alex." Orville rubbed his hands across his face, as if bracing himself for what was to come next from his mouth. He then looked at his wife. "Alex was killed in an automobile accident. I hope it really was just an accident."

"Oh my God!" exclaimed Mrs. Reid. "Oh my God!"

She got up and started walking towards the bedroom. "I'm going to take a nap. I need to take a nap. I wish you wouldn't leave the house. I have to take a nap."

John Walker's 12-year-old daughter, Caroline, called her mother at work. "There's a strange message from daddy on the answering machine. He left it yesterday. I guess you forgot to check it last night when you got home."

"Yes dear. I was tired. I saw patients all day."

"Well, I didn't want to erase it before telling you."

"What does it say?"

"All it says is 'I'm innocent and I love you.' Innocent of what, mom? Has dad been cheating on you? Is that why he went to Washington?"

"I don't know darling. I hope not. Why don't you hang up the phone and let me retrieve the message from the office here."?

"Okay mom, bye."

"Goodbye, Caroline."

Kathy hung up the receiver and then dialed her home telephone number. After the third ring, she pushed the access code. "Hello Kathy. This is John. I cannot explain anything to you now. I just want to say that I am innocent and I love you."

"That's strange," Kathy said to herself after listening to the message. "Innocent of what? What bimbo has set the trap for you this time?"

That evening in their home, Kathy watched the network television news with her daughter Caroline, who was sitting at the kitchen table reading. Kathy was at the counter, next to the television, chopping vegetables.

"The FBI has put a Professor John Walker on its 'Ten Most Wanted List," said the anchor. Walker, a white supremacist, is wanted for the murder of an FBI agent who was monitoring the activities of white supremacy organizations." A mugshot of John was shown in the background of the news anchor.

"What?" exclaimed Caroline, as she stood to her feet. "That's a lie! Mother! Tell me that's a lie!"

Caroline began to cry. Her mother put her arms around her and consoled her. "It's a lie," said Kathy.

During a Friday morning coffee break, Jane was standing at the vending machine when she overheard her colleagues discussing the newspaper headline of the FBI manhunt for the white supremacist.

"They should just shoot him on the spot and save taxpayers the money of a costly trial," one of the lawyers said.

"Shoot him and not even think twice," said another one. "This is just proof that our work will never end - white supremacists killing FBI agents. Will Martin's dream ever be fulfilled?"

Jane, sipping her cup of coffee, looked over their shoulders and saw the headline, "FBI Manhunt Continues for White Supremacist John Walker."

"Let me see that please," she said quietly. As she read the story, she realized that something terrible had gone wrong. She left the room and called Michael.

"Hello Michael."

"Yes, Jane. I guess you've heard the news about John Walker."

"Is it true?"

"No. At least I hope not. I haven't had a chance to talk to Orville yet but I hope it's not true."

"Maybe you should talk to him," said Jane. "You don't know whether it's true or not. This stuff is so crazy! You don't know who to trust!"

"That's why we can't talk about this on the telephone. You never know who is listening."

"You're right, Michael."

"I'm going to call Orville this afternoon."

"That's a good idea. I'm glad you told me Michael. You know what?"

"No. What?"

"I think John Walker is innocent. I don't know him but based on what you said in that letter, it looks like he was framed."

"That's what I think. And I'm sure that's what Orville will say. Jane."

"What?"

"Let's make ourselves a promise."

"Yes."

"Let's promise to never talk about this over the telephone again."

"Sure, Michael. I'm sorry. I was just so worried about you."

"I understand. I love you Jane."

"I love you too Michael. Talk to you later."

Michael called Orville's home later that afternoon. Orville's wife picked up the telephone and answered it with an aged and cracking voice, "Y-e-s."

"Hello, Mrs. Reid?"

"Y-e-s."

"This is Michael Woods. Is Orville there please?"

Mrs. Reid began to sob.

"May I help you?" a man's voice then asked.

"Who is this?" asked Michael.

"This is NOPD. May I help you."

"Yes, I want to talk to Professor Reid. Is he there please?"

"Professor Reid is dead," said the officer. "He was killed less than an hour ago in a mugging right outside the house here. We're investigating the incident. Who is this?"

"I'm a friend," said Michael, swallowing his fear.

Mrs. Reid got back on the telephone. The elderly woman, doing her best to compose herself, began to weep aloud as her voice cracked.

"I am truly sorry Mrs. Reid," Michael said. "I pray that God will give you strength. Please let me know if I can be of any help. I'll talk to you later."

"We saw him attacked there in his driveway," one of Orville's neighbors told police, a neighbor who had since walked over to the house. "He had a grocery bag in his hand, had just gotten home from the store. They took his money and then they killed him!"

"Give me a description," said the officer.

"They were black, teenage boys. Two of'em," said the gray-haired neighbor in his 60s.

"It's horrible!" said the man's wife, standing next to her husband. "This is supposed to be a good neighborhood." The wife then went over to Mrs. Reid and put her arm around her to help comfort her.

The local news media reported the death as typical of the city's drug related crime problem. "The killing of a university professor is the latest in a string of murders that have now pushed the city's murder rate to 132 for the first three months of the year. We remain the murder capital of the United States," reported a local news anchor.

The field reporter covering the story interviewed a Loyola University sociologist who said "Poverty, drugs, and unemployment are the root cause of our city's crime statistics. As long as we remain the second poorest metropolitan area in the country, the young person on crack cocaine will continue to be our worst nightmare."

Home alone, Doris Neuhaus watched the same ten o'clock news. She admired the professor's misguided insight, as she sipped from a tall glass filled with scotch and ice. The doorbell rang. Doris placed her drink on the cocktail table and went to answer it. It was her friend, 14-year-old Roland. She opened the door and Roland hurriedly entered the house.

"Did you see the news?" he asked.

"I saw it," answered Doris, with a distant yet seductive smile. She grabbed her purse from the cocktail table, took out $200.00 in cash and handed it to the boy. Roland took off his right sneaker, put the money deep down in his sock below his ankle, and then put the shoe back on his foot. Doris intently observed his every motion.

Michael was afraid to leave his house. The fact that Jane had telephoned him terrified him. Michael could not stay cooped up in his house forever. It was the last day of Spring Break and he had to be back at work on Monday. Two Institute faculty members had died that week. Although he knew what Orville had told him was true, he did not know who all was involved. Was it only Barry Bonds? Were others involved as well? If so, which ones and how many? What happened to Tyrone? Was Bernstein's suicide not a suicide? These questions raced through Michael's mind.

Chapter Eight

Michael worshiped at the St. James Full Gospel Baptist Church on Sundays. It was a large church where congregants gave their all, in service and praise to God. On this day, "I Just Can't Stop Praising His Name," was being sung by all congregants as they raised their arms, clapped their hands, and let their praises to God flow freely.

"Please Lord. Please deliver me from the valley of the shadow of death," was Michael's silent prayer, as he stood at his pew, in the midst of this singing.

As Reverend Coleman stood up, the singing gradually tapered. Susie and Constance, as always, were singing in the choir. Their loud shouts of rhythm became low whispers of song. Freddie was playing the drums. His loud thumps became soft tapping. Kirk, standing to Michael's right in the congregation, lowered his arms from the air and placed praying hands before his face, as did Michael.

"Let us now hold hands for a moment of prayer and thanksgiving to our almighty God and to our lord and savior Jesus Christ," said the Reverend Coleman. Michael held hands with the two people beside him, Kirk to his right and a woman to his left.

"Lord, we thank you for allowing us to live another day," the Reverend went on. "We thank you for giving us a mind to want to serve you. Father, please draw us closer to you. Allow your holy spirit to guide us and direct us in your precious ways. Give us a hunger for more of you Lord! And, last but not least, please bless the delivery and inspiration of your word, in the name of your son Jesus Christ, amen."

The church ushers then came to the front of the church near the altar with collection baskets in hand. "Please be seated," said the Reverend. After the collection of tithes and offerings, the sermon began. As Michael sat listening to Reverend Coleman's inspired message, his mind raced back and forth from horrific fear to peace and safety. He was safe here, but what about tomorrow when he had to return to work? He would have to face people who might be murderous conspirators. What if he saw Barry Bonds? How many others were involved? He pondered.

"I'll just avoid everyone," Michael reasoned to himself. "I'll just stay in my office like I used to and not come out." Yet, Michael knew this was an unreasonable solution. He could not let anyone become suspicious of him. "How am I to act?" he then silently asked God. "Lord, how am I to act?" Michael knew he could not tell the Reverend Coleman. He could not tell Kirk or Freddie or Susie. He could not tell anyone.

"God tells me that there are some among you who are hurting!" proclaimed Reverend Coleman near the end of his sermon. "I have good news for you! God cares! God wants to comfort and cuddle you! He wants to show you that He loves you! Come to God. Come! Let God love you."

Michael stood up and walked towards the altar. So did a dozen other congregants. As soon as they reached the wooden altar, they got down on their knees, closed their eyes, and bowed their heads. The Reverend Coleman laid his hands on each of them, one at a time, and belted out a loud prayer to God on their behalf.

"Bless him Lord!" shouted the Reverend as he put the fullness of his hand on the top of Michael's head. "Walk with him! Protect him! Put a band of angels around him!"

As Michael folded his hands and his eyes remained closed, a single tear trickled down his cheek and he prayed. God's presence surrounded him. It gave him strength. He heard the choir softly singing, "The Lord is My Light and My Salvation. Whom Shall I Fear?"

"Thank you for touching them this morning Lord!" exclaimed Reverend Coleman, as he returned to the pulpit. "The Bible says that your sheep hear your voice. Let us all be sheep for your pasture."

Reverend Coleman took a handkerchief from his pocket and wiped the sweat from his face. He looked out at the congregation, gestured upward with both arms, and said, "Let us all stand and sing to the glory of God."

Still at the altar, Michael used his hands to wipe the tears from his face as he and the others stood up returned to their seats. Tears continued to run down many faces. A few people sobbed and two danced.

Michael returned to his seat, raised his arms toward heaven, and continued to worship God as he continued to feel God's presence. Meanwhile, two middle-aged women continued dancing down near the altar. They were vigorously stomping the floor with both feet simultaneously as God's spirit seemed to move them and as the congregation began to sing louder and louder with more and more rhythm. As the choir and congregation sang louder and faster, Michael lowered his arms and began clapping his hands and singing along.

The Reverend Coleman, who had been clapping his hands and praising God as well, walked over to the pulpit, handkerchief gripped tightly in his hand. He stood silently as the congregation and the choir quieted down. Michael saw the two dancing women gradually reconstitute themselves and make their way to their seats.

"Now, may we remain standing for the benediction," said the Reverend. Those congregants not already standing stood up. "May the Lord bless us and keep us until we meet again," said the Reverend. "Let the church say, amen."

"A-m-e-n," said the congregants, slowly but loudly, in rhythm with the musical instruments. Some of the congregants shook one another's hand before leaving the church. Others hugged each other.

"You wanna have lunch?" asked Kirk, as Michael shook his hand.

"Sure. Who else is going?"

"I don't know. Maybe just Constance."

"Why don't we do that," said Michael. "I don't feel like talking to a whole lot of people anyway."

"Something's bothering you isn't it?"

"Yes, it is."

"Well, we'll meet you at La Madeleine's in about half an hour. Maybe we can talk about it."

Michael enjoyed the company of Constance and Kirk at lunch. He wanted to make this lunch last as long as possible because he did not want to go home. But after an hour, Constance left.

"I've got to get going," she said with her usual smile. "The Outreach Committee is getting together later this week to discuss the mission trips. I'll let you know what choices we come up with."

"That's good. I prefer Destin or Daytona Beach," joked Kirk. "Keep telling them that."

"Bye Constance," said Michael.

"You wanna talk about what's bothering you?" asked Kirk.

"No. I can't talk about it. I can only depend on God. It seems like Reverend Coleman had already talked to God about it. I know he hadn't but it seemed like he had."

"Yeah, I know what you mean," chuckled Kirk. "When that happens to me, I say the Reverend's been reading my mail."

"That's the spiritual gift of discernment, right?" asked Michael.

"That's the Biblical definition of it. But we joke and say, Hey! You been reading my mail! What's funny is that the Reverend doesn't even know who is going through a problem. He just gets this discernment from God that someone is. He may not even know what the problem is. He just knows that someone's hurting. You know. There is no greater proof than that."

"What do you mean?" asked Michael.

"I mean that shows that God loves and cares for each of us more than anyone on this earth ever will."

"You're so right," said Michael. "You're so right." Michael then began to giggle, "Reading my mail, huh?"

"That's good," said Kirk. "You're laughing. That's good. Well, it's time for me to get going. But I'm sure you'll be all right. You're in good hands."

"Thanks for your concern," said Michael, as Kirk got up from the table. "I think I will just sit here awhile longer and have another iced coffee."

"Okay," said Kirk. "I'll call you later in the week and see how you're doing."

"Bye Kirk," said Michael.

"See you later buddy," said Kirk.

Thirty minutes later Michael left the restaurant. He drove home, quickly got of his car, and rushed into his house. He did not leave until the next morning when he had to go to work.

There was talk throughout the Institute about the unlikelihood of one faculty member being hunted by the FBI and two others dying over Spring Break. By 10:30 a.m., Gracie Mullen had put memos in every faculty member's mailbox, informing every one of the emergency meeting scheduled for later that day.

"Dr. Schultz has called an emergency meeting for this afternoon," Gracie told Michael, as he checked his mailbox following his morning class. "I guess you know about Dr. Walker and poor Drs. Sanchez and Reid."

Gracie began to cry. She put her hands over her face to conceal her tears, but there were too many to hide. The tears dripped down her face onto the typed letters lying on her desk.

"It's going to be all right, Gracie," said Michael as he sat down in the chair facing her desk.   Mitzie walked into the room. Michael stared at the floor. He didn't want to make eye contact with her or even see her face. Her presence alone was more than he could bear.

"We're all sad about these terrible tragedies," said Mitzie. "We will all work together to pull through this."

"Thanks Dr. Schultz," said Gracie. "I'm sure I'll be okay. This is just so crazy."

Michael was surprised at how cordial Mitzie sounded. He looked up and witnessed Mitzie's expression of concern. Mitzie certainly didn't seem bothered that Michael was in the room. She didn't even sneer at him.

"Yes, it is." Mitzie nodded in agreement. After collecting her mail and casually glancing at a couple of the letters, she turned her eyes again toward Gracie. "Please make sure everyone knows about the 4:30

meeting this afternoon. Please call anyone who doesn't pick up his or her mail."

"I will Dr. Schultz," said Gracie. Mitzie then left the room and returned to her office.

Michael had not witnessed Mitzie being so cordial in his presence since his first year at the Institute. And although she and Gracie were like oil and water, at that moment, they seemed to gel. Had the tragedies softened Mitzie? Had they forced Mitzie to realize there are more important things in life than power and influence?" He began to entertain the notion that perhaps Mitzie was not a member of the white supremacist group. Yet, she had done some terrible things to him. So, Michael still did not trust her.

"You're pretty shaken up over this too, aren't you?" asked Gracie.

"Yes. I am," replied Michael. He tapped the palm of his left hand with the mail he held in his right. "Hey, I'll talk to you later Gracie. I've got to get down to my office."

As Michael walked down the hall toward his office, he looked straight ahead. He did not want to make random eye contact with individuals sitting in their offices, looking out into the hallway. However, this time Michael did not shut his door. He left it wide open.

He sat at his desk, turned on his computer, and pretended to work. He could concentrate only on his troubles, though. He had a month and a half left at the Institute. Then he'd be unemployed with a huge mortgage, a ruined career, and a death squad nearby. He also had the lawsuit and if John Walker ever surfaced again, he'd have a good chance of winning it. That is, if he lived long enough to see a trial date.

He realized that he could not wait much longer for John Walker. He positioned his computer monitor so it was not facing the door. Using his anonymous and non-university e-mail account, he sent an email to Jane's similar account. He suggested that they go forth with their own investigation of the Institute.

"I'm all for it," replied Jane in her coded return message. "And, even if we find something concrete, I know we can't tell anyone right away. However, we'd have to tell Tisdale when the time is right."

Ditto," Michael emailed back to Jane. "If we find something, we can tell her when you come down in June. Maybe then we'll have substantiated it. Right now, John Walker looks like the only one who can substantiate anything. Be careful, Jane. I love you."

At the 4:30 faculty meeting, Michael sat next to Doris Neuhaus. He could tell that Doris was pleasantly surprised. She immediately struck up a conversation with him.

"Hello Michael. How are you dealing with all of this?"

"As best I can, I guess," replied Michael. "I know this is a shock to everyone here."

"Michael," said Doris, "I do apologize for not being a friend to you during your grievance hearings. It's just that I was afraid for my own job. Now that it's all over, please let me be the friend that I should have been all along."

"I only have a month left here," responded Michael.

"That doesn't matter," said Doris. "Let's get together and talk sometime. I'd like that."

"I'll let you know when I have some free time," responded Michael. "You know, with all the changes taking place in my life - the job situation, postponing the wedding and all - it's hard."

"I know," said Doris, smiling. "That's why I want to finally be a friend. You can talk to me about it."

Michael knew nothing of Doris' white supremacist affiliation. That is not to say that he was not suspicious of her. Michael was now suspicious of all the professors at the Institute. Tyrone's disappearance made him even more suspicious of Doris than he otherwise would have been.

Michael did not want to attend this faculty meeting or see these people, but he came to the meeting because he did not want his colleagues to suspect that he knew something. Even though four chairs to Michael's left remained empty, this was the first time in more than a year that Michael felt like a part of the faculty.

Halfway through the meeting, in walked Professor Henry Murphy. All eyes were momentarily on this middle-aged professor with thinning blonde hair and casual clothes. Henry was the only professor left at the

Institute who was a part of John Walker's circle. Michael's heart sank when Murphy not only sat beside him but shook his hand, and patted him on the back.

"How you doing, Mike?" asked Murphy, as if he and Michael were buddies.

Michael smiled and said, "I'm okay."

Michael did not know if Murphy knew of the white supremacist activities. Orville had not told him which professors were working with him and John. Michael just assumed that Alex Sanchez was involved because he was now dead. As Murphy sat down, all eyes turned again to Mitzie.

"As I was saying," she reiterated, "We need to put out a press release stating that we had no knowledge of John's association with the racist organization, and that it was something that he kept hidden from us. We need to issue this release immediately. The administration says it has to be out in time for the Associated Press deadline this evening. This will allow newspapers, both national and international, to carry it in tomorrow morning's editions. CNN will also be at this press conference."

"What about the local television stations?" asked Doris.

"The University Public Relations Office held a news conference this morning for the local media," responded Schultz. "I talked to PR and this is the official line we are to give the national media."

"Why don't they just handle the national media too?" asked Elliott Nussmeyer.

"The administration wants the academic unit that worked most closely with Walker to deny knowledge of these ties," answered Mitzie. "That's why it's important to have a second press conference. The public relations office and the administration insist that the news release come directly from the Institute and not the administration or public relations."

"In other words," responded Ralph Lee, "if we didn't know of it, how was the administration to know of it? This gets us both off the hot seat."

"Right," said Mitzie.

Stan Tullock was tapping his chin with his right thumb. Barney Holtz and Matt Kohl were also intensely absorbing every word being said. The expression on their faces revealed how serious they considered the matter at hand.

"Get you off the hot seat, huh?" exclaimed Henry Murphy, to everyone's surprise. "That is like throwing salt on the open wound. Isn't it?" Henry laughed. "You've got a racial discrimination lawsuit against you and now this. Wow! I couldn't have written a better script myself!"

"This is not the time for internal squabbles," responded Stan Tullock, removing his thumb from his chin and placing his hand on the conference table. "This is the time for us to work together and pull through this."

"Thank you, Stan," said Mitzie. "I'll have Gracie retype the press release, if necessary, and fax copies to the 20 media outlets listed on the second page. They will have it before this evening's press conference, which, by the way, is scheduled for eight o'clock. Copies of the press release are here on the table. Look over it and let me know what you think."

Matt Kohl, sitting to Mitzie's immediate right, reached for and grabbed the press release stack. He took one and passed the rest to the other faculty members.

"Will you be taking questions at the press conference?" asked Doris.

"Yes. Again, the administration insists that this be an Institute for Public Policy news conference. So, you are welcomed and encouraged to come back for it."

Michael almost left the meeting after Henry Murphy's outburst. "Why did Henry do that?" Michael silently asked himself. Michael could tell that Murphy was angry and didn't care who knew it. But what was really going on inside Murphy's head? Henry should know that John is innocent, Michael reasoned to himself. If so, why did Henry make such a comment? On the other hand, maybe Henry knows nothing of the investigation and therefore only believes what he read in the press. Or, maybe Henry only wants them to think that he knows nothing of the investigation. Maybe he does know that John is innocent. Maybe he is just playing it safe.

"Any objections?" asked Mitzie.

There were no objections. Everyone remained silent.

"Well, that press release will be distributed as written," said Mitzie. "Again, we are all shocked and saddened by these events. I will proceed as soon as possible in setting up memorial funds for both the Sanchez and Reid families."

"Any word on replacements?" asked Kohl.

"The provost office told me this morning that we will be able to keep both lines. This is sad," said Mitzie. "But, we will pull through it."

Again, there were several seconds of silence.

"What about Walker's job," asked Barney Holtz.

"We haven't gotten any guarantee on that one yet," responded Mitzie. "However, I believe we'll get to keep it. I think the administration just wants to take care of the more immediate issue of safeguarding the university's reputation first."

"Yeah, we'd better keep it," remarked Tullock.

Suddenly, Michael caught Barry Bonds staring coldly in his direction. Was Bonds staring at Murphy or was he staring at both Murphy and Michael? Michael did not know. Michael tried not to notice Bonds or, at least, to give the impression that he didn't. He hoped Barry did not sense his fear or his anger.

"I want to thank you all for coming to this meeting," said Mitzie. "If there is nothing else, I guess we can adjourn."

Michael wanted to leave the conference room before Doris or Henry Murphy asked to spend more time with him. "I've got to go," he said suddenly to both of them. "I have to be home before 5:30. But, it was good talking to both of you again."

"I'll talk to you later," said Doris.

"Okay," said Murphy.

Doris' green eyes watched Michael getting up and leaving the room. Murphy sat in his seat for a while, then slowly got up and left.

That Tuesday morning from her Chicago office, Jane started on the investigation. She found that the FBI had nothing on anyone at the Institute except the missing John Walker. She decided to contact a friend at the Southern Poverty Law Center. Late that afternoon, the contact called her back and provided her with some useful information. The SPLC contact told Jane that several Institute members were secret supporters of the Sykes gubernatorial campaign while publicly denouncing him. Jane immediately emailed the information to Michael's anonymous email account.

Michael received the information at home when he turned on his computer that Tuesday night. He emailed Jane back. "I've received your information."

But it was not enough. Michael decided to contact the wives of the dead professors and ask to meet with them. He waited a couple of weeks before doing so in order to allow them time to adjust to their loss. When he finally called, using a downtown pay phone, he told them he wanted to express his condolences. He was hoping they would volunteer some information.

Unfortunately, the wives had completely accepted the official explanations for their husbands' deaths. "He died in a mugging outside the house here," said Mrs. Reid when Michael went to visit her.

"Do you think or have you heard that his death might some way be connected with those accusations about John Walker?" asked Michael.

"I hope not," said Mrs. Reid. "I don't want to talk about that. I begged him not to go outside. It's ironic, you know. I was worried that those people who killed Maurice might kill my husband. But he was killed by two teenage muggers."

"So, you think John is innocent?" asked Michael.

"Yes, I do, because Orville believed that he was innocent. John called Marguerite early that morning and told her he had been framed. He left the same message on our answering machine here. He would not kill Maurice unless he is really one of them and I don't think he is. I think they killed Maurice because he was onto them."

"That's interesting," responded Michael. "I can tell that you are truly his friend."

"This is a terrible thing," said Mrs. Reid.

The next day Michael called Mrs. Sanchez's house. Again, he used a downtown pay telephone.

"My husband was not involved in any of that!" exclaimed Marguerite. "He was killed in an automobile accident. John Walker is out of his mind!"

"You talked to Orville before he died?" asked Michael.

"Orville died in a mugging," responded Marguerite. "It was just a weird coincidence."

"Okay," said Michael. "I hope I didn't upset you. I just called to express my sympathy. Goodbye."

Michael then called Mrs. Bernstein. "Well, it's been more than two years," said Mrs. Bernstein. "You know, I've tried to move on with my life. I sold the house. My memory of finding him there was too painful."

"Do you think the situation involving John Walker had anything to do with Harry's death? Do you think it could have been more than suicide?"

"No," said Mrs. Bernstein. "I know you are African American and I read about your lawsuit in the newspaper. But I don't think you're going to get any mileage from the allegations against John. He and Harry were outsiders there, you know. It's hard for me to even fathom John Walker being a white supremacist. He and Kathy were at our home many times for dinner as we were at theirs. I've talked to Kathy and she is just devastated. The word is that John has been framed. As a friend of Kathy's, I have to support her in her position. I'm sorry Michael."

Realizing that the wives knew nothing, Michael went home and started making plans to move out of his office. He had to be out in three weeks. He began gathering empty boxes from the attic and putting them in the trunk of his car. Gradually, he moved everything from the office except for the computer, the desk, and the filing cabinets, which were not his. By May 16, 1990, Michael had completely moved out of his office. He stacked the numerous books he had brought home on the bookshelves in his home study. It was a sad moment for Michael. Yet, not having to go back to work made him feel safer.

Michael had only two things to look forward to. One was Jane's visit next month. The other was life. "If I am still alive," he reasoned, "perhaps they don't yet know that I know about them."

He turned on his computer and discovered he had a message from Jane's anonymous email account. "No one I talked to has ever even heard of the Society of White Aryan Nation," wrote Jane. "It's like the group doesn't even exist. The only person from the Institute I can connect to white supremacist groups is John Walker. But he didn't have enough influence to get you fired. He was an outsider.

"I still plan to be in New Orleans the first weekend in June. I'll arrive Friday morning. I suggest that you try to get a meeting scheduled with Tisdale. As I said before, I think we need to inform her of the little that we do know. Although it's inadmissible, at least she can ponder it."

Upon Jane's return to New Orleans, she and Michael presented Tisdale with the little they had. Tisdale took the information soberly.

"This should not be mentioned to anyone," she said, "whether they be black or white." She then looked at Jane and said, "I'm sure you know this is not enough. It's not a crime to contribute money to a campaign."

"I know," said Jane. "I know we can't make the leap from giving money to Sykes' campaign to job discrimination against Michael. They'll still say he was hostile and antagonistic and that's why they fired him."

"In addition," said Tisdale, "this white supremacist stuff is all hearsay. If we don't get information directly tying the other Institute professors to white supremacist activities and to the murders of the dead professors, it's worthless."

Jane nodded in agreement and then said, "John Walker! If he is alive, and if he cooperates, he's the key to a successful strategy. You agree?".

"Right," agreed Tisdale, "Let's just hope he's still alive." Tisdale turned to Michael and asked, "If he is alive, what are the chances of his contacting you?"

"He will eventually get in touch with me. I know he will," responded Michael, thinking aloud. "I just hope he is alive. I just hope he's waiting for the right time. Michael pondered for several more seconds and then asked, "What if I contact the FBI and relay to the agency that I believe it has been infiltrated by white supremacists? What if I say that these same white supremacists killed Broussard, their own fellow agent? What if I say they did it because they knew Broussard had uncovered a link between SWAN and the Institute for Public Policy and was on the verge of uncovering SWAN operatives inside the agency?

"You can't prove any of that," Tisdale responded.

"I know," Michael agreed. "However, maybe the FBI can. The only thing we can prove is the professors' campaign support of Donald Sykes."

"Okay," said Tisdale. "But only if it's done anonymously."

That weekend at the house, Michael and Jane composed an anonymous letter which Jane took back to Chicago. The next day she drove to Milwaukee where she mailed it to FBI Director Louis Silverman. The letter said, "John Walker was in no way responsible for Maurice Broussard's death because he was working with Broussard on the investigation of SWAN operatives at the Institute for Public Policy." The letter also stated that "Walker's New Orleans associates who also knew of the investigation were all killed within days of Broussard's death and Walker's framing."

Throughout the summer, Michael continued to send anonymous electronic messages to the FBI Director. Michael hoped to at least alert Silverman to the possibility that the FBI was hunting the wrong man. Director Silverman took both the letter and the electronic messages under advisement and refused to discuss them with anyone but his closest associates. He would in good time decide whether the matter was worth investigating.

Chapter nine

John Walker had made his way to southern Idaho. He had grown a beard and mustache, dyed his hair black, and traded his academic tweeds for cowboy boots and a Stetson hat. He went by the alias Buck Greene, a drifter from Montana, and he drove a 1972 Chevy Nova which he had purchased for $400 back in Washington, D.C.

While driving through Nebraska, he had spotted an abandoned vehicle alongside the highway with a Montana license plate. He stopped and removed the plate from the vehicle and placed it underneath the back seat of the Nova. He figured it would come in handy later on. No one in Idaho would be suspicious of a car with Montana license plate.

He had been in Idaho for two months working as a ranch hand. The owner of the ranch was a member of the Idaho Militia and had gotten John involved as well. John had been in the militia for only couple of weeks when he was approached by three men after a weekly meeting.

"We've been watching you. The future of America depends on people like us taking our country back from the Jew dogs, the jack-booted thugs with guns, the white scabs, and their subhuman nigger experiments," said a man named Bill. Bill and the other two men all carried assault rifles. They were dressed in army fatigues, had bearded faces, and they wore black military style boots.

This was the moment John hoped he had been waiting for. "You know," said John. "You are right. Those damn scabs, coons, spics and hymies are stealing our country away from us God-fearing Americans. That's why I am in the militia."

"The militia is only a start," said a second man.

"Right," said Bill, "there is something bigger that's for people like us. We refuse to wait for the damn government to trip up and make a mistake. We are offensive, not defensive."

Bill then aimed his rifle at a target on a tree, hitting a bulls-eye. He looked at John, studying his every motion.

"Tell me more," said John.

"We'll be by the ranch tonight to pick you up. There's a meeting at 11 o'clock. Be ready."

"I'll be waiting," John told the men.

As John hoped, it was a monthly meeting of the local chapter of the highly secretive Society of White Aryan Nation (SWAN). John was recruited through the local chapter and made plans to attend the annual Gathering during the week of July 4th in northern Idaho.

One week before the Gathering, unknownst to John Walker, the Orleans University Board of Regents inducted a new president. It was a media event which championed equal opportunity and highlighted the university's commitment to workplace diversity. Mitzie Schultz was named the university's fiftieth president. Two days earlier, Stan Tullock had been appointed Director of the Institute for Public Policy.

At home in his den, Michael read the newspaper story about the induction ceremony and Mitzie's appointment. The newspaper report also included a sidebar on Stan Tullock being pegged to lead the Institute for Public Policy. At the top of the page were two large photographs of Mitzie at the induction ceremony. Smaller ones of Tullock dominated the bottom of the page. Michael felt as if the university had slapped him in the face all over again.

By the week of the Fourth of July, John had made his way to northern Idaho with five of his militia brothers. He had finally reached his destination, the place where he hoped to find information that would allow him to convince the FBI that it was chasing the wrong man.

If not for the SWAN banners and pictures of Adolf Hitler hanging in the background, one could easily mistake the Gathering for a family reunion - though one at which no cameras were allowed. There were small groups of people wandering here and there among the picnic tables. John was sure that somewhere in this crowd there did exist family reunions of distant cousins, great aunts and uncles, and long-lost relatives enjoying themselves under the warm sun.

He savored the aromas of grilled chicken and barbecued beef. He saw kites flying and people riding in hot air balloons. Individuals gathered for special events in eleven large tents.

John saw many strange faces during the week-long event. Every now and then he'd see a familiar one. He only hoped he was not recognizable.

On day one, a medium-sized woman in her late 40s with stringy brown hair, approached John. She walked up to him as he was observing a group of people near a food stand.

"Hello, cowboy," she said.

"You talking to me?" asked John, as he turned, and looked at the woman.

"Sure, you're cowboy, aren't ya?"

"I work on a ranch, so I guess I am."

"You do any ride'n?" she asked, sexily.

John smiled. He could tell she was cheap. But he didn't mind cheap.

"I'm Lucille and I'm from Tennessee. What's your name?"

"I'm Buck Greene. I work on a ranch down in southern Idaho." Lucille wiggled her shoulders.

John and Lucille spent the day together eating and drinking. She introduced John to two of her friends who were sitting on sleeping bags under a shade tree.

"Come on over here and sit down with us," said the woman with a bottle of beer in her hand and a barbeque plate lying in front of her. "Who's your friend?"

"This is Buck," said Lucille, as she and John walked over to the shade tree. "Buck and I just met. Buck, this is Lola and Ben. They're friends of mine from way back. We're all southern."

"Hello Buck," said Lola. "This here is my husband."

John could tell that if Ben was not inebriated, he was at least halfway there. He seemed to be having difficulty keeping his eyes open and his speech was slurred.

"We got plenty of food here and plenty of beer in this ice chest," muttered Ben.

"Yeah, you can keep our spot safe if we have to go and restock," said Lola.

"If there's any restocking, we'll go and do it," said John, as he and Lucille sat down on the ground next to Lola and Ben.

Lola was very much like Lucille. She was southern and she spoke with a country twain. Ben, in like manner, was coarse and rough around the edges, rustic in the way John was striving to be.

"My family bloodline runs deep into Old Dixie," said Lucille in a slow, west Tennessee drawl. "You know my third cousin is a big professor down there in New Orleans. He's here somewhere."

"What's his name?" John asked.

"Ralph Lee. You know we can trace our family tree way back to Pulaski right after the War. That's when our great grandpa Granville helped found the Klan."

"The Ku Klux Klan?" John asked.

"What other kinda Klan is there? You stupid or somp'n?" asked Lucille. "Ralph's side of the family settled down in Alabama, down near Decatur. Mine stayed in Tennessee. You know Pulaski is right on that Alabama-Tennessee line so it's not like they went that far away."

After a several hours John went to get more beer. When he returned to the shade tree, he found Ben stretched out on his back, asleep on the grass. Ben was snoring, his pot-belly was noticeably inflating and deflating with every breath. His polyester shirt was pulled up above his crusty navel.

"He'll sleep it off and be as good as new around six o'clock," said Lola.

"Well, just keep this for what me and Lucille drunk of yours," said John.

"Well thanks," said Lola. Why don't we walk around some and check out some more stuff?

Ben'll be okay here by himself. I'll be back before he wakes up anyway. Just put the beer in the cooler."

After walking around for a while, the three went back to the shade tree and found Ben just beginning to awake. So, they talked some more until evening grew even later.

"I'm inviting you to the cabin," said Lucille to John. "I get lonely there all by myself."

"I'll gladly keep you company sugar-pie," replied John, as he massaged the back of Lucille's neck.

"Oooh! That sure does feel good," uttered Lucille, as she pulled herself up from the ground. "I can hardly wait."

"Ya'll have a good time," said Lola.

"Enjoy yourself," said Ben. "Nice meet'n ya."

John spent the night with Lucille at the one room cabin. He was lonely and she had made him horny. John got out of bed early the next morning. He had started getting dressed when Lucille awoke.

"Leaving so soon?" she asked.

"Yeah, I've got work to do for my boss at the Gathering. Thanks for a good time."

"My pleasure," replied Lucille, as she watched John pulling up his jeans and buttoning up his shirt. "Give me a minute, if you want me to join ya."

"Well, I tell ya, this is something I need to do alone. So, I won't be able to spend any more days with you. But I'd be happy to meet you in the evening for a little get together."

"Well, if you put it like that," wistfully replied Lucille, "I can only say one thing. Just don't keep me wait'n too long, cowboy."

Lucille was still in bed. The sheet was pulled down to her waist. Her left leg was arched and slightly swaying. Her breasts, and the lines on her face, were sagging as the fresh morning sunlight burst through the thin, linen curtains.

As John walked out of that cabin door, he was glad to be away from Lucille. She represented everything he detested in life but was simultaneously being accused of.

He bought an endless cup of coffee and a couple of newspapers at the Aryan Coffee Shop which was located in one of the tents. He chose the *Spokane Daily Herald* because it was from the nearest city with a population of over 100,000. Spokane was just 50 miles away. The newspaper featured a front-page story about FBI fugitive John Walker and linked him to Aryan Nation, the neo-Nazi group headquartered in Hayden Lake, Idaho, just a few miles away from where the Gathering was being held. John could not believe how off-base the Spokane newspaper story was. The headline read: "Aryan Nation Member Sought in Slaying of FBI Agent."

It was as if the newspaper had deliberately made-up information knowing that a fugitive would not come forth and demand a retraction. John knew he had had no contact with Aryan Nation or any of its members unless he had unknowingly met some of them at the SWAN Gathering.

Furthermore, he and Maurice Broussard had no basis for linking anyone at the Institute for Public Policy to Aryan Nation. If journalists were licensed, John reasoned, *The Spokane Daily Herald* editors and reporters should lose their licenses forever. The only thing not false about the story was his name was correctly spelled under his clean-shaven FBI mugshot.

John tossed the paper and bought *The Denver Post*. The *Post* ran a much smaller story which pretty much stayed in line with the FBI reports. It simply stated "John Walker, the suspected white supremacist wanted for the murder of an FBI agent investigating white hate groups, is still at large..." John began to browse the displays. He spent about fifteen minutes at each one. Displays were put on by state delegations and they included sizable amounts of reading materials and videos.

Slightly before noon, as John stood in line to buy lunch at an outdoor stand, he was shocked to see way ahead of him in the line, Mitzie Schultz and her husband, millionaire businessman Dieter Schultz. Also, in the same line and directly behind the Schultzes, were Matt Kohl with his wife Carol, and Donald Sykes with his two teenage daughters.

After this group paid for their burgers, hot dogs, and beer, they began to walk towards the delegation tents. John realized he would have to postpone getting his own lunch. Following this group was more important. Deeply involved in a serious conversation with Matt Kohl, was a middle-aged woman whom John did not recognize. Her forceful presence suggested that she was a leader. As she walked beside Kohl, she continued to talk expressively. She seemed to be trying to convince him of something. John later heard Sykes call the woman Mattie.

Before long the group stopped at a large picnic table. Seated and standing nearby were Elliott Nussmeyer, Ralph Lee, Barry Bonds, Barney Holtz, Stan Tullock, Mark Vandenberg, Doris Neuhaus, and others.

A banner attached overhead read: "Louisiana and Mississippi delegations." Hanging above it was another banner. It was blue and it had the picture of a large, white swan majestically centered on it. Centered underneath the large swan was the acronym "SWAN" in large, white, bold and capital letters. Fifty bleeding red stars aligned the edges of the banner. This "SWAN" banner was a smaller version of an even larger one which hung over the grand stand.

John was surprised that SWAN had penetrated the heart and soul of the Institute for Public Policy. At most, he had assumed that only one or two people were involved. This blew him away. He was determined to get pictures. He had to have proof.

John had stuck a disposable 35 mm camera inside the crown of his hat and punctured a small round hole in the hat right in front of the camera lens. He took off the hat and pretended to fan his face while snapping pictures. He made sure he got pictures of the SWAN banners in the background.

John was amazed at the amount of admiration Sykes received from Institute professors. Sykes was clearly as much their hero as he was a hero to the "white trash" they openly accused his followers of being. On the other hand, John sensed that Sykes' overall level of importance was not elevated. Like the rest of those at the Gathering, Sykes was simply a foot soldier in SWAN's greater mission.

Later that afternoon John made his way over to the grand stand where the giant red, white and blue "SWAN" banner hung. Several high-profile speakers were about to be featured. A giant video screen hung at the back of the huge stage. It was showing the accomplishments of the speakers.

This was how John learned of Mitzie Shultz's ascendency to the office of president of Orleans University and Stan Tullock replacing her as director of the Institute for Public Policy. The video tape of Mitzie's induction ceremony was run immediately preceding her brief but cogent speech. John was beginning to think that Mitzie's speech was simply a rehash of her press conferences back in New Orleans. It reminded him of her speaking to the news media and updating them on her latest public opinion polls. However, Mitzie's conclusion departed markedly from the type of comments made by her during press conferences. John had never heard Mitzie talk like this before.

"The secret Society of White Aryan Nation and the Institute for Public Policy have one and the same goal," proclaimed Mitzie. "And beginning this day, the old and prestigious Orleans University has achieved this goal as well. It has achieved salvation! One more victory! One more victory toward the total awakening of a fallen America! Salvation will come to this fallen gem. And, when it comes, it will have come because of fallen America's purification and sanctification from the filth of the nonwhite and defiled races!"

The entire crowd applauded Mitzie's proclamation. Some yelled. The less dignified ones jumped up and down and stomped the ground with their feet. Some were swinging their arms in the air as they turned their entire bodies around in circles. However, the more dignified ones simply applauded to the top of their lungs.

The other speech John wanted to hear and get pictures of was that of Donald Sykes. Those pictures, he knew, would be very interesting to the people of the State of Louisiana where Sykes was running for governor. Sykes was not scheduled to speak until the last day of the Gathering, still three days away, so John would have to wait.

"Where've you been?" asked Bill, as he came up behind John with a barbecued chicken breast in his hand and barbecue sauce in his beard. "We were looking for you last night and yesterday. We wanted to introduce you around. Don't wander off."

"I'm not going anywhere," said John. "I wanna hear this city councilman speak. He's a professor and lawyer too. Policy studies, it says up there on the video screen."

"Yeah," said Bill. "As I told you. We are armed. We're armed intellectually, militarily, and politically. We are America's salvation."

A small balding man with a full beard wearing round wire-rimmed eyeglasses walked up on the stage. The preceding video screen had introduced him as Lawrence Stanton, dean of the College of Policy Studies at Spokane College and a newly elected member of the Spokane City Council. It had also shown tape from his political campaign and subsequent victory party.

"My election to the city council of the largest city between Minneapolis and Seattle is great news for the Inland Empire, consisting of eastern Washington, Montana, and the great state of Idaho!" The sea of faces in the crowd cheered.

"My election is a seed that has been planted. It is a seed for greater and greater things to come. Yet, as I sit on the city council of the Inland Empire's capital city, I don't have to look that far to see how the nigger race has attempted its stranglehold on this great white city. I only have to look down city council chambers to see that a nigger woman has wormed her way onto the governing body of one of the most racially pure cities in this country.

"This nigger woman is there because of the defiled policies of a fallen national government. She is there because of the racist affirmative action policies in the American automobile industry. She is in our great city because the National Motors Corporation forced clean and decent white people to sell their new car dealership to this nigra woman's black husband. How much longer will this go on? How much longer will God-fearing white Americans stand idly by while the Jews, the blacks, the Hispanics, the Asians, the Indians, and other non-pure groups stake their claim on our God-given inheritance? I say that beginning this day, the end of standing idly by has ended!"

The crowd cheered and Stanton paused. John could see him soaking up the accolades from the crowd. As the cheering quieted down, Stanton began to talk again. "That day has ended because new seeds have been planted and the harvest is on its way.

"In conclusion, the mongoloids, the nonwhite races, and the white scabs have long thought of me as one of their liberal friends. And they continue to do so. But the time will come when the 50 bleeding red stars will stop their hemorrhage. They will become white! When that day arrives, those who have defiled our country, white and nonwhite, Jew and non-Jew, nigger and spic, will pay a terrible and unforgiving price. They will beg for mercy but mercy will flee them!"

The crowd cheered in ecstasy. Because Bill was standing next to him, John did not take a photograph of the city councilman delivering his speech. Although the photograph wouldn't have helped John clear his name, John at least hoped that most Spokane voters would be shocked if they knew their newly elected councilman was a hate monger. John would have loved to have sent the photograph to the misguided *Spokane Daily Herald*.

"Over here," said Bill. Bill gestured for John to follow him over to where two men and a woman were standing. John followed Bill over. "This is Daniel Black. He's president of the Montana Power and Light Company. Dan, this in Buck Greene. He's a new recruit. He's one of us."

"Hello Greene," said Daniel Black.

"Hello," responded John, as he shook the quiet, intelligent man's hand. Daniel Black was establishment. John felt it.

"This is my wife Sheryl and my brother Don," Daniel said to John.

"Your twin brother, I assume?" inquired John.

"Yeah, that's right," answered Dan.

"Hello," said the wife.

"How ya doing," said the brother. The brother had a more casual demeanor and casual attire than Daniel, who was dressed in cotton slacks, a button-down cotton polo shirt, and tassel loafers.

"Where you from?" Daniel asked John.

"Montana is where I've lived most my life. But I was born in Arizona."

"That's good," said Daniel. "That's good."

The wife smiled. The brother nodded. John could see that they were all impressed with him, but he didn't know why. Was his intelligence somehow seeping through his attempt at portraying himself as a rustic ranch hand? Maybe he was doing a good job portraying himself as a rustic.

By day four of the Gathering, John had satisfied Bill's need to show him off as his trophy recruit. Finally, he had more time to himself. While wandering through the crowd near the grand stand, he decided to remove his hat and take more pictures. As usual, he cautiously looked around to make sure no one saw what he was doing. In the crowd, he saw the two men who had chased him into the back alley in Washington, D.C. He only hoped the two men did not see him. He quickly snapped their picture and then put his hat back on his head. The two men were beginning to stare in his direction. He pretended not to notice them.

John slowly began to walk away from the grandstand. He walked as if he were wandering aimlessly through the crowd, but John had a definite destination in mind. He was headed for the exit gate.

On his way to the car, he thought about mailing the disposal camera to the FBI. However, he realized he didn't know how far up the supremacist infiltration went. Furthermore, even if the men he had just seen worked for the FBI, the agency might not be alarmed to see its agents at the Gathering since the agency was investigating white hate groups.

So, as John was making the six hour drive back to the ranch in southern Idaho, he decided to mail the camera and film to Michael Woods. Michael, he felt, was the only person he could trust with something this important.

John decided to leave Idaho that day. He told his boss he was moving on and wanted his final pay. He received his cash pay and left.

Beau Lapiere and Mike Rogers had begun asking around about the suspicious character they had seen. They eventually stumbled across Ben and Lola, still sitting under the shade tree. Lucille's friends thought the man Beau and Rogers were describing sounded like Buck Greene. They became even more certain after Beau showed them a photo of a clean-shaven John Walker. This was so interesting that Lola and Ben stood up to talk to the strangers.

"Why ya'll looking for him?" asked Ben.

"Oh, he's just a buddy of ours," replied Rogers. "He's been keeping a low profile. That is, if you know what we mean."

Beau and Rogers did not mention Walker's name or show the FBI wanted poster to the couple. That's because the agents didn't want to draw attention to themselves or be forced to answer deeper questions as to why they were looking for Walker. But the couple made the connection anyway.

"So, that's the guy we've been hearing about in the news, huh?" said Ben, who was now shirtless, wearing dirty cuff-off shorts. "You know, he does look like the fella who was with Lucille."

"Who's Lucille?" asked Beau.

"She's from Tennessee," said Lola. "I don't think he's from Tennessee though. I think he told us he was from Montana."

"How can we find your friend Lucille?" asked Rogers.

"She has a cabin," answered Lola. "It's cabin number 305. She ain't there though. You best wait til this evening to try finding her there."

The couple talking to Beau and Rogers had no cabin. Like many others at the Gathering, they camped out in their sleeping bags under the open sky.

"That's him!" exclaimed Lucille, when Beau and Rogers showed her the photograph of John Walker that evening in the rustic, one room cabin. "That's Buck! That's the one-night stand who stood me up! Hey! You know, in this picture he looks like that guy who killed the FBI agent. But that guy's a professor down in New Orleans like my cousin Ralph."

"He's one and the same person," responded Mike Rogers.

"Oh my!" said Lucille as she tossed the photo back down on the coffee table. "Well! I bet my cousin Ralph knows him. Why did he lie to me?"

"He just wants to lay low with all the news coverage and everything," said Rogers.

"Well, I can understand that," said Lucille. "I can understand that. But anyway, I'm mad at him! He should have told me who he was. And, he shouldn't have stood me up. He should have come back like he said he was going to."

Lucille, sitting across from Beau and Rogers, rested her left leg on the arm of the chair, lowered her right leg, and began pulling up her dress, allowing the two men on the sofa opposite her to see all that she wished them to see. They smiled at her.

"Well ma'am," said Rogers, "you know where he lives."

"He works on a ranch down in southern Idaho," wistfully replied Lucille. "At least, that's what he told me. That's all I know." Lucille then leaned back in the chair and stretched out her legs even more.

Now that Beau and Rogers had discovered John's alias, they decided to stop showing his photograph. This would allow them to continue looking for John as quietly as possible. They found Bill in one of the Inland Empire tents where Idaho delegates gathered.

"We're trying to find Buck Greene," said Rogers. "We hear he's an impressive new recruit. Can you tell us where he is?"

"He was with us all day yesterday but we haven't seen him today," said Bill. "What I can tell you is that he's a ranch hand at the Tri-Star Ranch north of Twin Falls. He fit in well with the militia so we recruited him. He's a Montana guy."

"He's working out quite well," added one of the other Idaho men.

"Well, maybe we'll run across him tomorrow," said Beau.

"He's a real smart fella," said Bill, "Real smart."

"I'm sure he is," said Rogers, as he and Beau turned to leave the tent. Beau smiled.

That same Friday evening, John stopped at a convenience store in Kemmerer, Wyoming to buy mailing materials, including a roll of postage stamps. He also bought six pre-packaged sandwiches, some canned food, candy bars, fruit, a carton of soft drinks and ice for his cooler. Before driving off and while sitting in his car beside the store, John composed a brief letter to Michael.

It read, "From John Walker. Both our lives may depend upon this. If I am still alive, I will contact you soon..." He put the letter and the disposable camera inside a small cardboard box, wrapped it several times in brown mailing paper, secured it with heavy duty mailing tape, and put $3.00 worth of postage stamps on it. He drove to a roadside mailbox on Kemmerer's Main Street, placed the package inside the mailbox, and headed east on Interstate 80.

Saturday morning was the last day of the Gathering. Rogers and Lapiere skipped the activities and paid a visit to the Tri-Star Ranch. Having left the Gathering, they now freely identified themselves as FBI agents and showed the ranch owner the official bureau photo of wanted fugitive John Walker.

"That's Buck Greene," said the rancher. "But he's already left. He took his final pay yesterday afternoon."

"Can you tell us what kind of car he is driving?" asked Beau.

"Yes, it's an old, beat up Chevy Nova, '72, I believe," answered the rancher.

"What about the license plate number?" asked Rogers.

"I have it written down in the house," said the rancher. "Give me a minute." "I always write down the license plate numbers of my work hands. You never know what they might do or steal."

The rancher came out of the house with a small notebook in his hand. "Let's see. Here it is. 239-AKY. That's it. 239-AKY. Montana plates," said the rancher.

"You've been a big help," said Rogers as he and Beau began to leave the ranch.

The rancher then yelled out from the porch of his house, "Even jack-booted thugs with guns have a right to live." The agents realized the rancher was referring to Maurice Broussard.

Once back in their vehicle, Rogers and Lapiere used their cellular telephone to notify FBI headquarters that they had spotted John Walker at a white supremacist meeting in Idaho. "We knew we'd find him here," Beau said. "He saw us and took off but we were able to secure a description of his vehicle and license plate number. We'll get him this time."

"Beau, a directive has gone out that Walker definitely be taken alive," said the agent on the speaker phone.

"Alive?" exclaimed Beau, "The son of a bitch killed a fellow agent."

Director Luis Silverman got on the phone. "Men, I want Walker alive. That's an order."

"Damn!" shouted Beau as he turned off his cellular phone. "Can you believe this shit?"

"We'll work around it," Rogers calmly replied. "Don't worry. We'll work around it."

It was Sunday in New Orleans. Michael's mother and his brother, Steve, were visiting for the Fourth of July weekend, along with Jane. Jane and Pearl had gone to church with Michael that morning. Steve, however, chose to stay home, sleep in, and enjoy himself by drinking beer out by the pool. When Jane, Pearl and Michael got back from church, they changed their clothes and went outside to the patio to prepare the grill. Steve was lying beside the pool in a white patio recliner with several empty beer cans next to him.

"That boy should've gone to church with us," said Pearl as she, Michael and Jane were setting up the grill. "Lord, I wish he'd turned out more like his big brother. Now, he says he's gone quit school. Says he wants to play in a band. Says he wants to move to Memphis." She went into the kitchen.

"You two are quite the opposites, aren't you?" asked Jane, standing beside the grill, next to Michael.

"That's right," replied Michael, as he rearranged the charcoal and then lit it. "As a matter of fact, we have relatives back in Tutwiler who say the only thing Steve and I have in common is our mother."

"Oh, that's funny," said Jane, as she and Michael took a seat at the patio table, and allowed the charcoal to burn down. "My sister Lisa and I look alike, talk alike, walk alike and pretty much like the same things."

Jane then reached over and squeezed Michael's arm, "Wouldn't it be nice," she said, "if we could get married, have children, and live a normal life?"

"You know, I want that more than anything," responded Michael, as he looked into her eyes. "But we've already discussed it. I think getting married right now would be a terrible mistake."

"Oh, you two make such a pretty couple," said Pearl, as she came out of the house with two plates of meat.   Steve jumped off the diving board and into the pool's deep end, making a loud splash.

Although Pearl and Steve knew of Michael's lawsuit against the Institute and Orleans University, they knew nothing of the white supremacist activities. And, for the time being, Michael knew it was best to keep it that way, for his own safety and for theirs. He sat there and watched Steve swim.

On Tuesday, while home alone, and after going for an afternoon swim himself, Michael checked the mailbox on his front porch. Piled in with unwanted bills, late payment notices, and disconnect notices was a package with a Wyoming postmark but no return address. Michael became suspicious.

"Is this a bomb?" he asked himself. He called the New Orleans police.

"I just got this package out of my mailbox and I think it's a bomb."

"Why would someone send you a bomb?" asked the dispatcher.

"I can't say," responded Michael. His voice cracking.

"Don't open the package," advised the dispatcher. "Lay it on a flat surface in an open area outside of the house. I'll dispatch someone as soon as possible. What's the location?"

"I'm at 1050 River Oaks Drive," said Michael.

Michael took the package around back of the house and placed it on the concrete near the swimming pool. He slowly backed away from it, went inside his house, and put on jeans and a shirt. He then went out front and waited for the officers to arrive.

As soon as the police cruiser drove up, Michael went out to the driveway and talked to them. "Thanks for coming so fast," said Michael.

"What do we have here?" asked one of the officers.

"It's around back by the pool," replied Michael. "Follow me."

Michael took the two officers to the back of the house. "There, there it is," said Michael, pointing to the brown package laying on the concrete patio.

"Hey, you mind if we use this?" asked the first officer, grabbing one of the long-handled poles used to collect leaves from the pool.

"No, please, go ahead," answered Michael.

The officer grabbed the pole and lifted the package into its net. He dipped it in water for several minutes.

"Now, let's see what we have," said the officer. He placed the package back on the concrete surface and carefully opened it with tools he and his partner had brought with them. "It's only a disposable camera and a letter," said the officer, as he began to open the package.

"I believe that's an invasion of privacy," interjected Michael. The officer handed the letter and camera to Michael. Upon reading the life and death message from John Walker, Michael was tempted to tell the officers everything but he remembered what Tisdale had said. In addition, there was always the possibility that the police department itself was infiltrated. Michael realized it was too risky.

"Thank you for coming out," Michael said to the officers, "I apologize if I've overreacted to receiving this package."

"Do you have any reason to suspect that someone would send you a bomb?" asked the second officer.

"No," said Michael. "I just know of someone who received a similar package which turned out to be a bomb."

"Well, don't worry about it," said the first officer. "It's our job." The two officers then left the premises.

Michael immediately took the film to a 24-hour facility to have it developed. He hoped the water had not damaged it. Meanwhile, he placed the wet letter outside on the patio table for one hour so the sun could dry it, weighing it down with rocks from the flower garden.

That evening he couldn't sleep. He double checked the locks on his windows and doors. He got his .38 caliber pistol out of the attic, loaded it, and placed it on his nightstand. "What could possibly be on that film?" he asked himself. He got up and started to email Jane. Then he changed his mind. Perhaps he needed to guard her safety. First, he needed to know what on was that film. Next, he would go to Tisdale. Perhaps then he would tell Jane.

The next day Michael picked up the film. He did not open the envelope until he was home and behind locked doors. Fear gripped his soul as he observed the photo that showed a SWAN banner hanging over the heads of his former colleagues. In several of the photos, Mitzie Schultz, Matt Kohl and others seemed enthralled by the company of Donald Sykes. In another photo, Mitzie was gently touching Sykes' arm.

Once seeing the photographs, Michael realized the urgency of having copies made, which he did. One set was placed with his attorney.

A second set was mailed to Jane. A third set was sent to his mother. Along with each set of photos, Michael included a copy of John's letter. He also wrote a letter to his mother. In it, he asked that she not mention what she knew to anyone, not even Steve.

Chapter Ten

After hiding out for four days in an abandoned gold mine 30 miles west of Cheyenne, John Walker decided it was time he headed to New Orleans. He hoped that by now Michael had received the disposable camera he sent to him and had had the film developed. He knew he and Michael, more than anyone else alive, had the most to gain by exposing SWAN. Even more so, he hoped the SWAN operatives and FBI assassins were unaware of Michael's knowledge of them. With this hope, John drove south on Interstate 25.

He assumed his New Orleans home was now staked out and his telephone bugged, so he chose not to telephone his wife and daughter. Instead, he sent them mail with no return address.

"I am still alive. I am still innocent. And, I now have information to prove my innocence," he wrote to his wife Kathy while still hiding out in Wyoming. "However, I must now come up with a plan to bring it to light. Meanwhile, please remain calm. Continue about your business as if you haven't heard from me. This is crucial for your own safety and for Caroline's. Give Caroline my love. I will contact you again soon. Love John." John mailed the letter early that Wednesday morning, before daybreak, in Cheyenne.

An hour later, as he headed south on I-25, he saw smoke seeping through the steering wheel of his '72 nova. Hoping that it was nothing, John continued to drive. Soon smoke was seeping through other openings in the Nova's front panel. It was coming through the radio buttons, the air conditioner vents, and every other button and opening in the car's dashboard panel.

Thinking the car was on fire, John drove it onto the median and turned off the engine. As soon as he stopped the car, smoke started gushing up from out of the hood of the car. He opened the hood and found the radiator cap partially melted as smoke poured from it. The car was dead. He was surprised it had served him as long as it had.

It was 5:30 in the morning and John knew he had to push the car out of sight before daylight broke. He only had moments to work with. Not too far down the highway was an exit sign which he could barely see. As he pushed the car in its direction, he could see the sign more clearly. It read, Deer Crossing exit 1 mile. Fort Collins 5 miles.

John pushed the car for what seemed like forever until he reached the Deer Crossing exit ramp. He then got in and coasted down the ramp. Once at the bottom of the ramp and onto a two-lane country road, he pushed the vehicle into a wooded area out of sight. He strapped on his backpack and started walking south on the interstate, towards Denver.

It wasn't long before rush hour traffic started speeding by him. The motorists did not seem to notice John. He was as unimportant as the wild flowers growing beside the road, plentiful today but gone tomorrow.

After walking for two hours, Walker realized that if someone did not give him a lift, he was not going to make it. His feet were heavy and so was his spirit. He put out his thumb. Forty minutes later, a pickup truck with two shot guns displayed in its back window pulled off onto the median ahead of John. John walked up to the truck and saw a bearded man, about 60 years old, sitting behind the steering wheel. John instantly thought of the Festus character on "Gunsmoke." Lying on the passenger side seat of the truck was an assault rifle. As John looked at it, the man picked up the weapon and placed it on the gun rack with the shot guns.

"I'm Buck Greene. My car broke down a ways back. I just need to get to Denver," John said.   "That's as far as I'm going," said the driver. Hop in." John got into the truck and the driver pulled off.

"You look kinda' familiar," said the driver. "You must be from round here?"

"I'm from Montana," John replied. "I was just at a meeting up in Idaho."

"I'm coming from Idaho myself. The SWAN meet'n. Is that where I saw ya?"

"Yes, I was there. The Nation never looked better."

"My name's Les Wiley by the way. Pleased to meet' ya."

"Pleased to meet you too," replied John. "I'm in need of some wheels. You know any place I can get my hands on some for a couple of hundred bucks?"

"I may know of a little place down near Colorado Springs. No questions asked." Les paused, he then looked at John's worn clothes. "You look like you're sorta down and out. We always help our own."

John and Les Wiley drove 70 miles south of Denver until they reached Colorado Springs. Wiley then turned west toward an old mining town. A man who looked like Les but larger and healthier came out of a large garage-like structure to greet them. It was evident to John that the man knew Les well. "I've gotta fella here who needs some wheels. Can you help him out?" Les asked, immediately after getting out of his truck.

"Anything for a friend," said the man, who patted Les on his back.

John then got out of the truck and shook the man's hand. "I'm Buck Greene," said John.

"I'm Joe," said the man.

Joe, Les Wiley, and John walked inside the large warehouse type garage. There were motorcycles, automobiles, motorboats, and an arsenal of weaponry.

"How much for the scooter?" John asked.

"Five hundred dollars. They don't depreciate as fast as the automobiles. There's greater demand for them."

John felt that was too much. He needed something cheaper. His face showed it.

"He's one of us," said Wiley. Let's do what we can to help him out."

"Where ya headed?" asked Joe.

"Arizona eventually," said John, "I've got a wife and kid there. I've been working as a ranch hand up in Idaho. Montana's my home."

"I tell ya what I'll do for ya. I'll let you have that '81 Escort there. It's a much better deal for three hundred dollars. You need a place to sleep tonight?"

"Yes, I can use a place," said John.

"There's a little motel 'bout 20 miles down the road. My brother owns it. Tell him I sentcha. My name's Joe. He'll knock off half the price."

John spent the rest of the day doing handy work for extra cash. At six o'clock, Joe and Wiley headed home and John was given more precise directions to the motel. However, John decided to get a head start to New Orleans instead.

He realized that depending upon how well networked SWAN was, the agents may have already uncovered his alias and be on his tracks. So, driving south, he turned his car radio to the Colorado Springs all-news station and listened for as long as possible. After about an hour, he was beyond the station's signal range. He turned the radio off and continued to drive for ten hours. Barely able to keep his eyelids open, he exited the interstate at 4 a.m. south of Truth or Consequences, New Mexico and made his way to a wooded area near Hillsboro. Shielding the car with tree branches, he slept.

Seven hours later it was 11 a.m. John awoke and found a local radio station.

"The FBI has found the '72 Chevy Nova abandoned by wanted fugitive John Walker," the reporter said. "The vehicle was discovered off I-25 near Fort Collins, Colorado. Those in the area are advised to be on the lookout for Walker who is considered armed and dangerous." After removing the branches from off his car, John pulled back onto the road and resumed his journey to New Orleans.

Beau Lapiere and Mike Rogers were already in Colorado Springs. They were headed to Joe's Salvage and Auto, a known hangout for white supremacists in Colorado.

Joe denied all knowledge when the agents showed him the FBI mugshot of John Walker. He excused himself to answer the phone and while he was inside the shop, he made a call.

"There are two fellas here, Les. They're FBI agents and they say they're in SWAN. They're looking for that fella you brought out here yesterday. They say his real name's Professor John Walker. They say he killed an FBI agent. What should I do, Les?"

"What did you say to them, Joe?"

"I told them I know nothing."

"You did the right thing. They say they're in still SWAN. But how do we know they aren't spying on us at the same time? If this Walker did kill the agent, the agent deserved to die."

"But they've been in SWAN since they were teenagers and this Walker is an unknown to us," responded Joe.

"Perhaps Greene has something on them," reasoned Les. "What if he knows they've been double-agents ever since they joined SWAN? What if he knows they're feeding information to the government? Even if his name is John Walker, he killed someone who may have been onto us. That's good. Don't you think?"

"I've gotta go Les. I see they're getting impatient out there."

Joe hung up the telephone and walked back outside. Beau and Rogers were sitting on a wooden bench peeling apples with their pocket knives.

"Who were you talking to in there?" asked Rogers.

Joe remained silent.

"Why do you wanna to protect this enemy of the Nation?" Beau asked.

"How is he an enemy?" inquired Joe.

"His true identity is Professor John Walker of New Orleans," Rogers replied. "He and his buddy Maurice Broussard uncovered our infiltration of various universities and government agencies. They were about to expose us."

"We killed Broussard and now we must kill Walker," said Beau. "Wanna tell us where he is?" Joe was starting to believe them.

"I don't know where he is. He stayed at my brother's motel last night. Said he was going to Arizona."

"We know he's not driving that Chevy Nova anymore so how's he gett'n around?" asked Rogers.

Joe hesitated. Then said, "I'm not sure."

"We'll be in the area until tomorrow night. I'm sure you'll think of something before then. When you do, give us a call," said Rogers, circling the mobile phone number on his Federal Bureau of Investigation business card. Rogers and Beau stared Joe down before leaving. Joe's uncertainty was now matched only by his desire to help. If only he knew who to help.

Early the next morning, a Friday, Wiley drove his pickup truck into the gravel parking lot of Joe's Salvage and Auto. In a rush, he jumped out of the truck, slammed the door shut, and walked hurriedly towards the garage entrance. Joe was getting underneath a 1966 Ford Mustang when he heard the bell ring, signaling that someone had entered his shop.

"Joe! Where are ya?" shouted Les.

"I'm over here by the black Mustang."

I've got something to tell ya Joe." Wiley walked over to his friend.

Joe pulled himself out from under the Mustang and stood up.

"This had better be good," he said to Les, holding a wrench and screwdriver in his hand.

"They were right Joe!" exclaimed Les. Les talked fast but in a low tone of voice. "They were right about Greene. The agents were right!"

"How do you know?" asked Joe.

"I called the Gulf States regional headquarters in Baton Rouge this morning to see what they had on John Walker of New Orleans. They told me John Walker used the alias Buck Greene. They say Walker is our enemy. They say we must stop him before he talks to the wrong people. Joe, Greene fits the description they gave me. Joe, we've been had!"

Joe went over to his desk and got Rogers' business card from the drawer.

Rogers and Beau were eating breakfast in Colorado Springs when the cellular phone rang. Rogers had just picked up a piece of syrup-soaked hot cake with his fork. Beau was lifting a piece of sausage patty and scrambled eggs to his mouth. As Rogers put the phone to his ear, he quickly took a swallow of orange juice.

"Hello, Mike Rogers."

"This is Joe at Joe's Salvage and Auto. I've got something for ya."

"Okay! That's what I like to hear. Stay put. We'll be there ASAP.

When the agents drove up, Joe ran outside to meet them. "Here," said Joe. "He's driving this here car. I sold it to him Wednesday." Joe handed a photo of the blue Escort to Mike Rogers. "Here. Look. The license plate number is on the back of this picture here."

"Why the fast turnaround?" asked Rogers, as he examined the photo of the car and the license plate number on the back.

"I gotta a friend who checked on some things after you left and found you were telling the truth. I'm sorry," said Joe. "I just hope I didn't do nothing to hurt the revolution. I just hope I didn't do nothing." Joe became speechless.

"Don't worry about it," responded the normally impatient Rogers. "A little dose of apprehension and suspicion is sometimes good for the revolution. It shows devotion and commitment. You've done the right thing in the end. That's what matters."

As John Walker drove east toward New Orleans, he kept the car radio tuned to all news stations whenever possible. A San Antonio radio station's "Morning Show" had as its top news story the Louisiana gubernatorial election results.

"Former white supremacist Donald Sykes has won the Louisiana gubernatorial primary by a landslide," said the announcer. "Sykes now faces Democrat Roy Robicheaux. Robicheaux left office seven years ago after being indicted but never convicted on extortion charges."

"You're speaking to the next governor of the great State of Louisiana," Sykes told the reporter. "The people of this great state know that my past is my past and not my present or my future. I call upon all Louisianians, black, white, and Latino, to join with me for victory in the November 3 runoff election."

As soon as John crossed the Louisiana state line, some six hours later, he began to see "Sykes for Governor" billboards. Even more prevalent were "Sykes for Governor" yard signs, bumper stickers, and posters attached to utility poles and any other stationary object. Some of the signs simply read "Sykes." John had forgotten how enthralled Louisianans were with this closet Nazi. As much as he wanted to prove his own innocence, he knew that he had to expose Sykes for what he really was.

As soon as he got to New Orleans, he would find a safe place to hide out. He would find a way to convince law enforcement officials that they were chasing the wrong man, that he was innocent and had killed no one. He could think of no better place to do this than in a courtroom with a judge, lawyers and witnesses present. However, he first had to contact Michael. He had to know that Michael was still alive, had the film he had sent to him, and was not under heavy surveillance by SWAN operatives.

What John did not know was that SWAN's elite command and the FBI were both already on the lookout for his '81 Escort. And both had a good idea of his whereabouts. When he had stopped for gas late Thursday afternoon in Ft. Stockton, Texas, the clerk had become suspicious of him and had double checked the FBI Most Wanted poster which was hanging on the service station wall.

"I don't know for sure but that could be him," said the attendant after calling the number on the wanted poster, only minutes after John drove away from the station. "I wrote down the license plate number. It's Colorado license plates and its 999-CKY. He was headed east on I-10 from Ft. Stockton, Texas."

John had also stopped for gas in Crowley, Louisiana. His license plate number was spotted by an officer in SWAN's elite command who just happened to be buying gasoline at the same convenience store. The officer made a mobile phone call and tailed John for an hour. After making a second phone call, the officer exited the interstate and drove west.

It was basic instinct that persuaded John Walker to bypass Baton Rouge. Suspecting that a SWAN regional office was located in the city, he decided to turn south off the interstate at the little town of Grosse

Tete and onto parish road 77. He stayed on parish roads until he reached New Orleans.

Once in New Orleans, he drove around until he spotted an abandoned building at the corner of Esplanade and North Rampart Streets. The windows were boarded up and the house was plastered with political campaign posters from years past.

Over grown banana trees covered the backyard, like a mini-jungle. John parked the car a couple of blocks away on a side street and removed the license plate. He walked back to the abandoned house and entered it through the rear of the building by removing two boards that had been nailed over a broken window. The hideout was perfect. It bordered the Faubourg Marigny and the Vieux Carre. There was at least a half dozen other boarded up houses in the vicinity, alternative housing in case of need.

Rogers and Beau arrived in New Orleans within hours of Walker. They summoned other members of SWAN's elite command and began combing the neighborhoods where they thought Walker was likely to seek refuge. They staked out his home for days. They searched the Quarter at night on foot. They searched uptown, the West Bank and parts of Jefferson Parish.

John mailed a letter to Michael his first night back in New Orleans, a Saturday, and requested that Michael call him on Wednesday from a pay phone. He specified the time of day and the telephone number of the pay phone where he would take the call.

He mailed a second letter to Kathy. In it he said, "This is to let you know I'm back in New Orleans. Although I now have proof of my innocence, it's too early for me to come forth. I need money. You cannot contact me. The house is probably staked out and you will be followed." He specified exactly how Kathy was to get the money to him.

In the letter to Michael, he wrote, "I hope you have received the package I mailed to you. I hope that you have secured it. Even better, I hope you have made copies for safe keeping. I'm sure you know that I am innocent. I now know Orville had the right hunch when he convinced me it was time to inform you about SWAN. If he hadn't, you probably would not trust me now. Anyway, I know your case is scheduled to go to trial soon. The courtroom would provide the safest place for me to reveal what I know. If the strategy works, it will vindicate me and be worth lots of money to you. Please discuss this with your attorney. I'm sure she knows how important it is to keep something like this secret. Call me as I have instructed."

Michael, reading the letter that Tuesday morning at home in his study, immediately telephoned Tisdale's office. He requested an urgent meeting for the next day, a Wednesday, around the same time he was to call John, at two o'clock.

That Tuesday afternoon, when she got home from work, Kathy parked her car in the driveway, as usual, and checked the mailbox before entering the house. There was a letter with no return address. She had come to take for granted that all letters with no return address were from John. However, she did not know that Mike Rogers and Beau Lapiere were watching her from their unmarked car. Kathy entered the house and wept as she read the letter.

"Mom! What's wrong?" asked Caroline, as she walked into the foyer after hearing her mother cry.

"Nothing darling," said Kathy, placing both her hand and the letter onto the foyer table, and bracing herself. "I'm just upset because of the situation with your daddy. He's going to be okay though. It's only a matter of time before it's all straightened out. It's only going to be a matter of time."

Kathy quickly picked up the letter from the foyer table, mixed it in with the other mail, and put it into her purse. "Caroline, I have to meet a patient tomorrow night at 9:30. It won't take long. I'll be back no later than 10:30. Will you be okay here alone?"

"Sure, mom," said Caroline. "You know I'll be okay. I'm not a baby."

The following day, Michael made his way to Tisdale's office for his meeting with the attorney.

"This is good. This is a good idea," she murmured as she read the letter John had sent to Michael several days earlier. "The trial starts in a week. I'm now convinced his coming forth will indeed exonerate him and win your case for you."

"Well, let's go and call him," said Michael. "He'll be in the vicinity of this pay phone number for the next 30 minutes. He said we are to use a pay phone to call him at this pay phone number."

"Let's go," said Tisdale. As Tisdale walked out of her office, she told her secretary to expect her back in time for her three o'clock appointment.

Michael and Tisdale walked to a payphone located inside the World Trade Center in downtown New Orleans because it had booths large enough for them both to fit into. As Michael dialed the number, Tisdale stood by.

"Hello," a suspicious voice answered.

"John?"

"Who is this?"

"This is Michael."

"Oh good. Michael. I recognize your voice."

"John. I had the film developed. I have copies secured. I talked to my attorney. She is right here. She is convinced that your plan will work."

"Oh wow!" responded John. "My life has been hell for the past six months. "God! I only hope that this hell will soon end."

"I'm sure it will," said Michael. "I'm sure it will."

"Let me talk to your attorney," said John. "That is, if she doesn't mind?"

"Here, he wants to talk to you," said Michael to Tisdale. "Is that okay?"

Tisdale took the receiver, "Hello, Professor Walker?"

"Yes."

"Hopefully we will soon put an end to all of this. As Michael just told you, I think your plan will work. We will get through this. We will vindicate your name and this hell of yours will finally be over."

"You don't know how good it feels to finally be able to talk to someone," said John. "The little things we take for granted in everyday life become the most important when we don't have them. But I guess I shouldn't waste any more time talking for talking's sake. So, how do you suggest we proceed with this from the angle of the trial?"

"I'll request permission to call an unnamed witness. If that doesn't work, I'll call you at the last minute, convincing the judge of the urgency of your testimony."

"That sounds workable. When?"

"We'll have to hold off until day two of the trial. Unless there are some unexpected continuances, that'll probably be at least one week from tomorrow. The trial starts a week from today."

"Let me to talk to Michael," John told Tisdale. Tisdale handed the phone to Michael inside the cramped phone booth. "She sounds like she's holding a winning hand, doesn't she?"

"Yes, she does," replied Michael.

"The wait will be the toughest part," said John. "But I'm sure I'll make it. It'll be worth it. We'll get'em good."

"Thanks to you John, we will. Where are you?"

"I don't think I should say until we're ready, next week."

"I understand," said Michael. "You stay safe. I'll call you again at this same number a week from today. And, I'll call at the same time. That is, unless I hear from you with other instructions."

"Sounds like a plan," agreed John.

Chapter Eleven

Kathy Walker arrived home late that Wednesday afternoon and checked her mailbox as usual. She was doing her best to keep up her routine as John had instructed in his letter. And, as usual, Mike Rogers and Beau Lapiere had followed her home in their unmarked vehicle.

Getting bored with the routine, the two decided to leave the stakeout that day at six o'clock. Usually, they would have returned after an hour or so. But this evening they did not. Continuing to watch the Walker house were two rookie agents secretly assigned to the case by Silverman. They were to keep tabs on Rogers and Lapiere but their major directive was to find John Walker.

At nine o'clock Kathy Walker left the house in her white Mercedes Benz 190D. She was followed by the two rookie agents in their brown unmarked Chrysler. Jeff Kemp and Keith Conlin were in their mid-20s, and both were temporarily stationed in the bureau's New Orleans District Office.

They followed Kathy as she drove downtown and parked in a public parking garage three blocks from the French Market. She took the elevator down to ground level and began to walk. Jeff Kemp followed her on foot and Keith remained in the Chrysler, parked four rows back from the Mercedes.

Kathy entered the open-air market just as shops were closing. When she stopped at the pay phone, Jeff crossed to the other side of Barracks Street to watch her from afar.

Kathy took a match box from her purse, placed it on the bottom panel of the phone booth and stuck chewing gum from her mouth to the top of the matchbox. She lit a cigarette and made a phone call.

As Kathy was talking, Jeff noticed her hand going underneath the phone booth's bottom panel. When Kathy hung up the phone, she walked back towards the parking garage.

Jeff contacted Keith by cellular phone. "It looks like Mrs. Walker may have stuck something underneath the phone booth. I'm going to check it out."

Jeff put the cell phone back into his pocket and crossed the street. Not wanting to look suspicious in case John Walker was watching him, he dialed Keith on the pay phone. He then felt underneath the bottom panel of the phone booth and touched the match box.

"She's left something here for him all right. I'll stay here and see if he shows up."

"Okay, you do that," responded Keith. "I'll keep an eye out for her on this end."

Kathy walked back to the garage, got into the car, and drove home. Keith Conlin followed her in the brown Chrysler.

At midnight, Jeff Kemp was sitting on the sidewalk with a 16-ounce cup of beer in his hand. He had bought it at the watering hole at the end of the block, in plain view of where he sat. The loud noise from the bar helped to keep him company. The rookie agent could have easily been taken for just another drunk with no place to go.

As Jeff sipped on his beer, John Walker walked up to the phone booth. It was about a mile from Walker's hideout. He picked up the receiver and pretended to make a phone call while removing the match box from underneath the phone booth panel. He walked back to the abandoned house, with Jeff following him from a distance on foot.

Once John had entered the house by the back door, Jeff telephoned Keith. "He showed up at midnight. Looks like he took whatever his wife left there for him. Best of all, he's led me to this abandoned house at the corner of Esplanade and North Rampart. I have a good hunch this is where he is staying."

"Did he go inside?"

"Yes, he went inside."

"Good job. You think we should move our stakeout over there then?"

"Yes. Our number one directive was to find him and we've done it. We'll notify Silverman tomorrow morning. He'll tell us what to do next."

"I'm on my way," said Keith.

Jeff walked across the street, to the side of the house, and waited for Keith at the corner bus stop. The dimly lit stop provided an excellent spot to remain inconspicuous while watching out for Keith and John Walker. Once Keith arrived, the brown Chrysler easily blended in with other cars parked on the street, in the mostly residential neighborhood.

The rookie agents had been ordered by FBI Director Luis Silverman not to discuss their operation with anyone at the agency but him. When they called Silverman the next morning, he told them to continue their stakeout of the abandoned house until they received further instructions. "What about our keeping tabs on Lapiere and Rogers?" asked Jeff.

"Eventually they'll show up there too. But don't worry about them for now. What's important is that I know everything I can about Walker's comings and goings. If he meets with anyone or talks to anyone or if he even sneezes too loudly, I want to know about it. Got that, Kemp?"

"We got it, sir."

"How did you find him?" asked Silverman.

"We think he may have mailed a letter to his wife and told her to leave some money or something at this phone booth. We followed her last night. Walker didn't show up until three hours later. But I could tell she had stuck this match box to the bottom of the phone booth. So, I waited for him there. Keith followed her in the car."

"Good job," said Silverman. "Keep watching Walker, and let me know what else you find out."

The agents staked out the abandoned house and followed Walker for four days straight. Keith would remain in the car and watch the house while Jeff would follow Walker on foot. Walker seemed to talk to no one except for an occasional phone call. He made routine trips to one of two nearby corner grocery stores. There too he hardly talked to anyone, including the cashiers.

It was now Tuesday and Barbara Tisdale was in her office with Michael. They were discussing John's surprise appearance in the courtroom that was to happen in just two days. "I realize he might be arrested, but I hope it won't be until after he's testified," said Tisdale.

"If the judge allows him to," Michael reminded her.

"Let's say our prayers," responded Tisdale. "The one thing on our side here is that Judge Katherine Sims is liberal and black. If she thinks there's the slightest indication of white supremacist activity, she'll give us a very long leash with this."

"Maybe our prayers have been answered, then," said Michael. "But I'm not counting on her giving us the long leash. I've learned the hard way that things are not always as they appear."

"Unfortunately, you're right again," said Tisdale.

"Okay," said Michael. "I'm to pick John up at ten o'clock Thursday morning. He said he'll be waiting outside the abandoned house at 1415 Rampart Street, underneath the banana trees, and out of plain view. I'll drive him to the courthouse and signal you that we have arrived by beeping your pager."

"That's our plan," said Tisdale. "Any other questions?"

"No," said Michael, as he stood up and gathered his notes.

"Good. I'll see you Thursday morning. Call me if need be."

"I always do," said Michael. "And, I want to thank you again for taking this case and working on it so diligently. I know you didn't have to do it. You could have been like all the other attorneys in town I contacted. You could have turned me down."

"I had a feeling about this one," reflected Tisdale, leaning back in her chair. "I just had this strong feeling. And, this time I was right."

After days of waiting, Luis Silverman decided it was about time Walker was brought in. Agents Jeff Kemp and Keith Conlin got Silverman's phone call Wednesday morning while sitting in the stakeout car.

"Move in very early tomorrow morning and apprehend Walker while he sleeps," said Silverman. "Take him directly to the district office for processing and preliminary questioning. Don't let him out of either of your sights for one split second. Is that clear?"

"Yes, sir," said Jeff.

"After questioning, I want the three of you on the first plane here. Absolutely nothing is to happen to him. He has information too important to us. Is that clear?"

"We understand," said Jeff.

"Good," said Silverman. "I'll see you tomorrow afternoon."

"I heard it all," said Keith, sitting behind the steering wheel. "What'll we do in the meantime?"

"Well, there's no longer any need for us to just sit here in this hot car. Let's get something to eat. Any place that has air conditioning. Roll up the windows and turn on the AC."

"Okay," said Keith. "You know, we should get some sleep too, since we'll probably be spending most of the night here at the stakeout."

"Yeah, you're right," said Jeff. "Let's go home after we eat. What time do you think we should get back to the stakeout?

"How does eight o'clock sound?"

"That's sounds about right," agreed Jeff. "Now, roll up these windows and turn on that AC."

After a quick lunch at a Faubourg Marigny eatery, Keith dropped Jeff off at his apartment in Jefferson Parish, and went home to his own apartment, which was just around the corner from Jeff's. Having slept all afternoon and into the early evening, Jeff awoke around seven o'clock, showered, and walked to Keith's apartment right before eight o'clock. He knocked on Keith's door.

"I was just about to call you," said Keith, as he opened the door, and while buttoning up his shirt. "Sorry we're running a little late. Just give me a couple of more minutes."

"Hey man," said Jeff as he walked into Keith's apartment. I have an idea."

"What?" said Keith.

"We don't have to apprehend Walker for about ten hours. We don't know when we'll be back in New Orleans and it's been all work since we came down here. Whatta you say we explore the French Quarter tonight? We can hang out there at least until midnight. That'll give us plenty of time to stake out the house and arrest Walker by five or six o'clock tomorrow morning."

"Yeah," replied Keith, "but we have to be absolutely certain that he and he alone is in that house. We can't afford any surprises. I say the earlier we're at the house the better. We have to cover our asses."

"Keith. Listen to me," instructed Jeff. "Am I mistaken or was it Keith Conlin who has been sitting in that car for more than a week watching John Walker do the same damn thing day in and day out? Is this the same Keith Conlin who has never seen anyone else go inside that house but John Walker? Is this the same Keith Conlin who has never witnessed John Walker meeting with anyone?

"Okay, you may be right," said Keith. "I guess spending a little time in the Quarter won't hurt anything."

"Okay!" said Jeff. "Get dressed and let's get down to the Quarter. It's party time."

Taking advantage of what might be their last night in New Orleans for a while, the two rookie agents made their way from street to street from club to strip joint in the Quarter. They lost track of time at a karaoke club called the Cat's Meow, thanks to two flirtatious women named Helen and Sue. The two agents were standing up with their backs to the bar, and observing the singers on stage, when Jeff caught a sexy blonde smiling at him and giving him a seductive stare from down on the floor. Before they knew it, the four of them were singing and dancing on stage.

Michael was at home this night preparing for what might be the biggest day of his life. He finished reading over his notes and reviewing copies of Walker's SWAN photos. He planned to turn in early. It was important, he felt, that he got a good night's sleep.

At this very same time David Piston, a graduate student at the Institute, encountered John Walker at a grocery store at the corner of Decatur Street and Barracks. Walker was standing at the counter.

Piston, who usually wore khakis and tailored shirts, was dressed in black leather and walking by when he spotted John from the sidewalk. When Walker left the store, he saw what he perceived to be a group of skinheads not realizing that one of them was David Piston.

As Walker turned away from the store, Piston said to the rest of his party, "I have some business to take care of. I'll have to catch up with you later at the club." He followed Walker for about 20 minutes until he saw him go into an abandoned building. It was one thirty in the morning.

David wrote down the address. He then went back and joined his party at the Black Crystal, a club that catered primarily to punk rockers and skinheads. The only light was from tiny colored light bulbs in the black ceiling. The clientele mostly wore leather pants, leather jackets, and leather boots, but tonight the leather jackets were not in evidence as the men were shirtless in the heat. The women wore loose fitting black and white linen garments with military style leather boots. Many had shaved their heads. Nose rings, tongue rings, navel rings, an assortment of tattoos, black lip and eye makeup, and dyed black hair adorned men and women alike. Some had spider webs tattooed on their elbows.

David and his friends locked arms in a circle. All six then stuck out their tongues, exposing their silver studs and tongue rings. They unlocked their arms and continued to dance, some as couples and some alone, to the thumping head banger music.

By 2:30 a.m., and at the karaoke club, Keith was trying to get Jeff to leave, but he was no match for Helen who thought the party was just getting started.

At 7:30 a.m., David Piston and his party were just leaving the Black Crystal. Piston walked alone through the empty streets of the French Quarter, trying to shield his eyes from the unwelcome morning sun. Sanitation workers and restaurant delivery drivers were just beginning their morning routines. Piston made it to his car, got in, and drove to his apartment near the university. He arrived home at eight o'clock.

Upon entering the front door of his apartment, he slung his leather jacket onto the shabby sofa. The "White Power" tattoo on his upper right arm was highlighted by lightning bolts coming through it. On his upper left arm was the tattoo of a human skull with bones crossed underneath it.

Piston went into the kitchen and got a gallon jug of water from the refrigerator. He turned it up and began to drink. He then took two pills from a prescription bottle which was sitting on the kitchen counter, put them into his mouth, swallowed, and drank more water.

Looking half alive, Piston walked into his bedroom and threw himself onto his unmade bed. He tossed and turned as if he could not allow himself to fall asleep. He reached down and grabbed the telephone which lay beside his bed on the floor amidst scattered dirty clothes. He dialed the SWAN regional headquarters in Baton Rouge.

"This is David Piston. I know where John Walker is hiding out." He paused. "He's in the abandoned building at 1415 Rampart Street, at the corner of Esplanade. I followed him there last night." He then hung up the phone, curled into a fetal position, and went to sleep.

Michael had been awake since 7:30 a.m. After showering and getting dressed he called Tisdale at 8:45. "Everything is on schedule," he told her.

"Good," said Tisdale, "I'll see you at the courthouse at 10:30."

Jeff and Keith were waking up in Helen and Sue's hotel room. Helen and Sue were not there, but before leaving, the women had gone through the agents' personal items, looking for something.

"Oh my God! Look what time it is!" exclaimed Keith.

"Don't panic!" responded Jeff, as he removed a pair of pantyhose from around his neck. "We know where he is. He's not going anywhere. If we don't get him this morning, we'll get him tonight." The agents showered, got dressed, and set out for John Walker's hideout.

"I wonder why the girls left without letting us know anything," Keith asked while driving the car.

"Who knows?" replied Jeff. "Maybe they had a six o'clock flight. Or maybe they're married. Either way, let's just be thankful for the good time."

Michael drove down St. Charles Avenue, across Canal Street and towards the Faubourg Marigny. He hoped John Walker would be waiting for him. He crossed Esplanade and pulled up to the back of the old house. It was 9:58 a.m. He waited for a couple of minutes. Then he parked his car around the corner and walked to the back of the building.

The back door was missing. He walked into the abandoned building and saw the broken-down door lying to the side of the entrance. As he walked toward the center of the room, he could see takeout food boxes near a place where someone had been sleeping.

He then heard a scream. It was John's voice! "NO!!!"

"You son of a bitch!"

"He's dead! Let's get out of here!"

Michael tried not to breathe. He slowly backed up against a wall. The wooden floor beneath him creaked.

"What's that?" he heard one of the men say.

Michael sensed that the men were turning around to enter the room of the house where he was standing. He heard another creak. This time it did not come from the floor where he was standing but from another room.

"Stay here. I'll go check it out," one of the men said, and then, "It's nothing." Michael heard the two men leave the house.

Cautiously Michael entered what apparently had once been a dining room. He saw John's body hanging from a chandelier hook. The men had attempted to hang John to make his death look like a suicide. Eventually he had continued to struggle. Beau had stabbed him in the heart and stomach. John's clothes were torn and bloodied from the attack.

Michael peeped out the window and saw the men get into a car marked Federal Bureau of Investigation. He ran out the back door to his own car to follow the men. He could think of nothing else.

By this time Jeff and Keith drove up to stakeout the house. "It's ten after ten. Let's wait and see if Walker comes out or goes in. That'll be our signal," said Jeff.

"I guess you're right," agreed Keith. "We don't have to worry. His car is still down the block."

Sitting on the passenger side, Jeff opened up the glove compartment and took out two pairs of sunglasses. "You need a pair of these?" he asked Keith.

"Yes, I do," answered Keith.

Michael followed Rogers and Beau on I-10 West as far as LaPlace. By then he had memorized their license plate number. He headed back to New Orleans.

It was eleven o'clock and Barbara Tisdale, expecting Michael and John at 10:30, had had to explain to Judge Katherine Sims why the plaintiff had not shown up nor the pivotal witness Tisdale had promised. Tisdale was lucky. The judge recessed court until 1:00 p.m.

It was 11:30 before Michael got back to New Orleans. He contacted Tisdale by pay phone, and explained to her what had happened. Tisdale told Michael to meet her at the abandoned house and she immediately called the police. Two NOPD officers arrived and entered the abandoned house before Tisdale and Michael got there. Jeff and Keith followed the officers in, and flashed their FBI badges.

"This is a federal matter," Jeff informed the officers.

"I think this is a dead matter," one of the officers replied, "as in dead body." He gestured over his shoulder.

Jeff and Keith rushed into the room where John's body was still hanging. The rookie agents were dumbfounded. All they could do was stand around and try to look useful. Shortly thereafter, Michael and Tisdale entered the front yard.

"I'm the one who called the police," Tisdale said to the officer now guarding the entrance to the house.

"You're an attorney?" asked the officer.

"Yes," said Tisdale. "This is my client. He found the body when he was here this morning to give the deceased a ride to the courthouse."

"You'll have to give us a statement," said the officer.

"We'll be glad to," said Tisdale.

After providing initial statements in the front yard of the abandoned house, Tisdale agreed that she and Michael would show up at police headquarters the next day to give additional statements, if need be.

Meanwhile rookie agent Jeff Kemp was talking to FBI Director Luis Silverman on his cellular phone. "Walker's dead," said Jeff. "He must have been dead when we arrived here this morning. We were waiting in our car when we saw New Orleans police drive up and enter the house. They found him dead."

"What time did you arrive at the stakeout?" asked Silverman.

"Ten minutes after ten, sir."

"What time did you leave there last night?"

"We were not there last night, sir."

"Where were you?"

"We were in the French Quarter, sir. However, an eyewitness saw the two men who committed the murder take off in a bureau vehicle this morning around ten o'clock. The description of the men does fit Rogers and Lapiere."

"I see," said Silverman. "I see. Well, stay there and assist the NOPD as long as they need you, then be on the next plane to Washington."

The rookies spent the rest of the day collaborating with the local police and sharing information with them on Walker's movements in the week preceding his death. The next day they flew to Washington and provided Silverman with a full account of their operation. This included information on Mike Rogers and Beau Lapiere.

Silverman now realized that Walker was indeed innocent. He knew that if the rookies had not goofed up, Walker would now be a vital link in helping the agency to resume its investigation of SWAN, an investigation which for all intents and purposes, had come to a halt.

The rookies had no plausible explanation as to why they were late arriving at their stakeout on the morning of Walker's death. They were severely reprimanded.

Chapter Twelve

Barbara Tisdale rushed into the courtroom. Leland Metzger, lead counsel for the defense sat with Mitzie Schultz, Mickey Calabrese, and Hodge Williams at the defense table. They watched Tisdale hurry to the plaintiff's table although the plaintiff was nowhere to be to be seen.

"Attorney Tisdale, please be advised that you have worn the patience of this court very thin. Do you have an explanation for the delays you have caused and the unprofessional behavior you have exhibited?" Judge Sims's impatience was audible.

"May I please approach the bench, your honor?"

"You may," responded Judge Sims. "Counsel for the defense will also approach the bench."

Tisdale walked up to the bench from the plaintiff's table. Leland Metzger was there waiting for her with a smile. He had gotten there first. Tisdale ignored him and looked at Judge Sims.

"Your honor, the plaintiff's crucial witness will not be here this afternoon because he was killed sometime this morning."

"Who was this witness?" asked Judge Sims.

"He is the accused white supremacist and fugitive from justice John Walker."

"You realize he would have been arrested on the spot, don't you counselor?"

"I realize that, your honor."

"What relevance does John Walker, dead or alive, have to do with this case?" asked Attorney Metzger.

"What is your answer?" the judge asked Tisdale.

"John Walker insisted that he was innocent, your honor. He insisted that he had no affiliation with any racist group but was framed because he knew too much." Tears began to come to Tisdale's eyes. She paused, wiped her eyes, and composed herself.

"Your honor, he insisted he was framed by white supremacists, some of whom are professors at the Institute of Public Policy."

"What!" exclaimed Metzger.

"Please, counselor!" the judge silenced him. "We'll have to take this up in chambers."

As Judge Sims turned to inform the court, she would be having a brief discussion with counsel in her chambers, Leland Metzger's face reddened. Tisdale knew that if looks could kill she'd be a dead woman.

"This is all hearsay, and from someone who is not only a wanted fugitive but reportedly dead!" exclaimed Metzger as the three of them entered the judge's chambers.

"I agree," said Judge Sims. "But let's see where Ms. Tisdale is going with this."

"John Walker," said Tisdale, "was willing to testify that some of the professors disguised themselves as liberals and orchestrated the plaintiff's problems while the plaintiff was employed as a professor there."

"That's ludicrous!" angrily exclaimed Metzger. "I have never in my entire legal career heard such unsubstantiated garbage! Your honor! FBI reports show that John Walker was the only professor at the Institute with any ties to hate groups. Your honor, you are aware of the fine reputation the Institute has in civil rights policy."

"I am Counselor Metzger," said the judge. "Attorney Tisdale, please be advised that you have gone from sliding down hill to the bottom of the bottomless pit! I am leaning towards holding you in contempt of court for your behavior."

"I know how this sounds, your honor," responded Tisdale. "But I have reason to suspect that Walker was telling the truth. I ask that you please allow this trial to go forward so that the plaintiff and I may have the opportunity of convincing the court of such."

"Because I was called to the scene of the murder this morning, I have not had time to discuss an alternative strategy with my client." Tisdale's pager beeps. She looks at it and then turns it off. "He just walked into the courtroom moments ago. Your honor, I am pleading for a ten-minute recess so that I may discuss matters pertinent to his case with him."

"You don't have any other surprise witnesses for the court, do you?" asked Judge Sims.

"No, your honor."

"Does the defense object to this requested ten-minute recess?"

"No, your honor," said Metzger. "I am willing to go along with anything just to get this debacle over with."

"Well, let's get back out to the courtroom," said Judge Sims.

As the judge and two counselors reentered the courtroom, the spectators could be heard mumbling with anxious anticipation. Yet Matt Kohl, and his wife Carol, sitting on the first row behind the defense table, exhibited stern confidence. So did newly appointed university president Mitzie Schultz, Provost Mickey Calabrese, and former president Hodge Williams.

"There is going to be one more delay," said Judge Sims. "We will be taking a ten-minute recess. Afterwards, we hope to wrap this case up before the end of the day."

"We need to talk in private," Metzger said to President Schultz, as he briskly walked over to where she was seated. "Stan, Matt, you need to come too."

"Why can't we all come?" demanded Elliott Nussmeyer, sitting in the same row as Matt Kohl.

"We only have ten minutes," replied Metzger. "It's easier to explain the problem and develop a strategy if I'm only working with three people. Mitzie is now university president. Matt and Stan worked closely with Woods. We can fill the rest of you in later. Hurry! We don't have much time. Room C is empty. Let's go."

"Don't say anything, Michael," said Tisdale, as Michael scurried up to her. "Don't say anything until we are in Room A with the doors shut tight. C'mon! We only have ten minutes."

"What are we going to do?" begged Michael, as he and Tisdale sat on the back bench in empty Courtroom A."

"Now that we no longer have John Walker's eyewitness testimony, this entire case rests on your shoulders," responded Tisdale, as she took her copy of John's letter and the photographs from her brief case. "You are now your case. Our only hope is to try to enter this letter along with these photos as exhibits and hope the judge accepts them."

Tisdale was trying her best to exhibit confidence and self-assurance. The morning's events had gotten the best of Barbara Tisdale. As Michael's attorney, she felt she owed that much to him. But her tough exterior was being slowly peeled away, revealing the nervous woman inside. Tisdale knew civil law; she knew it well enough to recognize that she was facing the dragon. A single false move and her career would be history.

"A letter from an accused dead murderer won't appear that convincing, will it? Can it even be used as evidence?"

"That all depends," responded Tisdale. "The good thing is the defense doesn't know the letter or the pictures exist."

Tisdale placed the letter and photos on the bench beside Michael. "This is our bombshell. We have to get the maximum bang from it. If you are convincing enough, Sims may overrule any objection the defense raises. Michael, we are in the darkest tunnel. This is a longshot, but it is our only way out. If we lose this case, both our lives will be in danger."

"What about the long leash you said we could expect from Judge Sims?"

"Don't count on it," responded Tisdale. "As of now, she's definitely leaning towards ruling in favor of the Institute."

"Oh God," replied Michael. "Let's hope this works."

Meanwhile, in courtroom C, Leland Metzger stood before Mitzie, Matt Kohl, and Stan Tullock. "I've got bad news and good news," said Metzger, as he leaned against the front row railing. "The good news is that as of this morning, John Walker is no longer among the living."

Mitzie Schultz, sitting to Metzger's far left, quietly smiled. Matt Kohl and Stan Tullock smirked and began to relax in their seats.

"What's the bad news?" asked Kohl, as he crossed his legs at the ankle and leaned farther back in his seat.

"Unfortunately, Walker did make contact with Michael Woods before his death. He unloaded some nasty information to him. Depending on what kind of evidence they have to back it up with, it may be bad enough to undo the case. That is, if Sims buys it."

Mitzie's smile vanished. Her face grew still and tight with anger. Stan Tullock looked uneasy.

"What exactly do they know?" demanded Matt Kohl. He sat up straight with his feet firmly on the floor.

"Everything," said Metzger. "Everything. Tisdale claims that there are white supremacists at the Institute who deliberately orchestrated Woods' problems because he is black. She also says that Walker was framed because he knew too much. However, based on the meeting we just had in chambers; Sims isn't buying it. The judge is a friend of Russ Brown and she knows the good reputation the Institute has in civil rights. There's a good chance she'll rule it all hearsay. If she does, you win, and it's all behind you."

"That depends on whether they have supporting evidence," interjected Mitzie.

"You're right," agreed Metzger.

"How the hell can they have anything?" exclaimed Matt Kohl. "If they had anything, we'd know about it!"

"That is, unless they've been hiding it," responded Metzger. "But that's unlikely. It appears they staked their entire case on John Walker, a witness they were afraid to inform us about. Since he cannot show up, I believe their case has fallen apart."

"Even if we do win, it's not all over," responded Kohl. "Knowledge is power. If Woods knows and his attorney knows, it won't be long before others start believing them. The problem will have to be fixed."

"That's mop up work," smirked Metzger. "I have nothing to do with that."

Mitzie got the cellular phone from her purse. "Who are you calling?" asked Stan Tullock.

"We can't depend on Sims ruling it all hearsay," responded Mitzie. "We need a backup plan. Mike Rogers was investigating this for the FBI. We need him here to confirm that John Walker was the only professor at the Institute suspected of this type of activity."

"Excellent strategy!" proclaimed Metzger.

"Yes. I know," sarcastically replied Mitzie. "So, what do we need you for?"

Metzger briefly lowered his head. "I do my best," he responded. "I called you all in here because we all have input to give. And, it's working."

"Mike Rogers?"

"Yes."

"This is Mitzie Schultz from the Institute. Hey, we are in court. We know Walker is dead but unfortunately, he talked to Michael Woods. Although it's hearsay, Woods' attorney is about to argue that white supremacists at the Institute framed Walker and orchestrated Michael Woods' problems. We need you here to counter it all and make our case air tight."

"Okay," said Rogers. "But we're almost in Baton Rouge. It'll take us at least 45 minutes to get there."

"We'll wait," said Mitzie. "Just get here."

"Let me talk to him," said Metzger.

"Hello, Mike. This is Metzger. I just want to go over some things. We only have about five minutes before the trial resumes so listen carefully."

"I'm listening."

"Okay, you will testify about your investigation of Walker, a known right-wing extremist, whose ties to white supremacist groups triggered the ambush of agent Maurice Broussard. You will say that you and your partner, Lapiere, suspected Walker of murdering Harry Bernstein because Bernstein was Jewish and knew about Walker.

"You will say that Broussard had held off on apprehending Walker hoping that Walker would lead him to other infiltrators. Do you have all of that?"

"I've got it," said Rogers. "I'll go over it with Beau here as we drive to keep it fresh in our minds. Since it's the truth, it shouldn't be that hard to remember! Right?"

"You got it," said Metzger. "If we need you, we'll probably call you to the stand as soon as you arrive. If we don't need you, the trial will be over before you get here."

Barbara Tisdale and Michael Woods were back in the courtroom before Judge Sims, Leland Metzger and the other defendants arrived. Sims looked surprised to see Tisdale already there. As Sims sat down, she gave Tisdale a nod, as if Tisdale had finally done something right.

"Civil District Court, Division D, with the Honorable Judge Katherine M. Sims presiding is now in session," said the bailiff.

"You may call your witness," said Judge Sims to Tisdale.

"Your honor, I call Dr. Michael Woods to the stand."

Michael was sworn in.

"You may take the witness stand," said the judge.

"Please state your name for the record," asked Tisdale.

"My name is Michael Woods."

"Tell the court where you were employed and in what capacity between 1987 and 1990."

"I was employed as an assistant professor in the Institute for Public Policy at Orleans University."

"Why did you leave the Institute in 1990?"

"My contract was not renewed."

"Why was that?"

"I believe it was not renewed because of a climate of racial harassment of which I was subjected to. I believe the harassment was orchestrated by key professors. As a result, it spread to the student population as well."

"Do you mean professors harassed students or students harassed you?"

"Students harassed me through lies and accusations. Some of them didn't respect me because they knew the professors did not respect me."

"Do you have any evidence of this racial harassment that you believe existed?"

"Yes, I do."

"May I approach the witness your honor?"

"Yes, counselor," grudgingly replied Judge Sims.

Tisdale took from her brief case a copy of the letter and photos mailed to Michael from John Walker. She walked over to Michael and handed the items to him.

"Please tell the court what items you hold in your hand," stated Tisdale.

"I have a letter from the deceased John Walker. He sent it to me while running from the FBI. Also, in my hand are copies of the pictures he sent to me of Institute professors and FBI agents attending a white supremacist gathering in Idaho."

"The defense objects to the relevance of this material as well as to this line of questioning!" shouted Leland Metzger.

"Overruled!" said Sims. The judge's curiosity had been ignited. The grudging disposition she had shown earlier toward Tisdale had disappeared. Tisdale felt as though fresh air had blown into the room. Michael breathed a huge sigh of relief.

"Plaintiff enters the letter from the deceased as exhibit B and the corresponding photographs as exhibits C through G. I assure you, your honor," said Tisdale, "that these exhibits are directly tied to plaintiff's case and will be highly relevant to arguments made."

"The Court accepts plaintiff's exhibits B through G," said Sims.

"Dr. Woods, will you read the letter for the court please?" asked Tisdale.

"If I am still alive, I will contact you soon. Meanwhile, know that your dismissal from the Institute was conspired from the date of your hiring because of your race and because of the orchestrated undermining of affirmative action by those who pretend to support the policy."

The faces of several Institute professors in the courtroom were stone cold. Mitzie Schultz and Matt Kohl seemed to be grinding their teeth. The other professors, and their spouses, stared at Michael as if to sear his very soul.

"My life hangs in the balance," Michael read. "I am being pursued by the men in photo number one who are FBI agents and members of SWAN, the highly secretive Society of White Aryan Nation. They planned the assassination of agent Maurice Broussard because he had uncovered SWAN's infiltration of the Institute of Public Policy and SWAN's connection to Bernstein's death. The other photos show Institute of Public Policy professors present at SWAN's annual Idaho Gathering."

In walked agents Rogers and Lapiere. They seated themselves at the back of the courtroom. Michael gestured with his eyes for Tisdale to look behind her. As she turned, she saw the two men being seated.

"I am the only person alive with knowledge of SWAN's infiltration of the Institute and its connection to Bernstein's death," said Michael as he continued to read from John Walker's letter. "This is because within days of killing Broussard, SWAN operatives also killed two Institute professors who were onto them. These professors were Orville Reid and Alex Sanchez. I can expose SWAN's infiltration of the Institute, the FBI, and possibly other institutions of government."

"Are the two men pictured in exhibit B, or what the letter refers to as photo number one, in the courtroom?" asked Tisdale.

"Yes," replied Michael.

"Will you point them out please?"

"They are in the back of the room. They're on the back row -- my left side. They are the two men wearing the navy-blue suits. The one with red hair and the muscular one with brown hair."

"May the court recognize that the plaintiff has identified the subjects in exhibit B, your honor?"

"So recognized," responded Judge Sims. Judge Sims looked at the picture and then glanced at the agents. She then placed the picture aside.

"Are the subjects featured in exhibits C through G in the courtroom?" asked Tisdale.

"Yes, they are all seated at the defense table and immediately behind it. They are the woman with blonde hair seated at the defense table, Mitzie Schultz, all five people seated in row one, all five people seated in row two, and the man seated next to the aisle in row three."

"Order in the court!" exclaimed Judge Sims.

The whole courtroom was out of control as people began to talk among themselves. Judge Sims looked at the additional photos and then shook her head as if it were too much for her to digest. Psychology professor Carol Sweeney and Black Faculty and Staff Association President Erroll Fontenot, sitting across the courtroom on the plaintiff's side, couldn't restrain themselves.

"I knew it!" yelled Sweeney, as she stood up and pounded her fist on top of the bench in front of her. "I knew it!"

"I knew something was wrong over there at that Institute!" responded Fontenot, as he too stood up. "But, my God! I never knew it was this! My God!"

Urban Studies Professor Edna Auta, sitting next to Carol Sweeney and Urban Studies Dean Hebert, sitting next to Fontenot, were both awe-struck. Their mouths were open but no words came out. They simply looked silently in the direction of the defense table.

"I'm not one of them!" yelled out Henry Murphy as he stood up and moved away from where he had been sitting, next to Ralph Lee, in row three. "I tell all of you, I am not one of them. I've never been one of them. I was a friend of John Walker."

Russell Brown, the civil rights leader who had publicly supported the Institute throughout the trial, dropped his head in embarrassment as he sat next to the empty seat Henry Murphy had just vacated. At the defense table, Russ Brown's friend, Hodge Williams whose eyes had been opened, sat tense and silent. The man who always had an answer for everything now had no answer.

Provost Micky Calabrese was sitting between Hodge Williams and Mitzie Schultz. With both his elbows on the defense table, Calabrese covered his face with both his hands and lowered his head as if to hide himself from the reality that had just hit him like a cannon ball.

Mitzie refused to look at anyone. Doris Neuhaus, sitting on the second row, also lowered her eyes.

Judge Sims used her gavel to silence the confusion in the room. "I order all those named in Walker's letter and featured in these photos, including President Mitzie Schultz, be detained for questioning concerning conspiracy charges for the death of Harry Bernstein."

Several professors arose and attempted to rush out of the courtroom. Bailiffs swiftly apprehended all of them.

"You black bastard! You're a dead motherfucker!" yelled Stan Tullock at Michael, who was still in the witness chair.

"Arrest this man, now!" exclaimed Judge Sims.

"Don't be a fool!" Mitzie Schultz angrily instructed Stan Tullock, as he was escorted passed her in handcuffs.

Tisdale and Michael looked out at the courtroom fiasco. They had done their job. The plan had worked even without John Walker being alive to carry it through. Although Michael felt sad for John Walker, he was relieved the truth was finally out. He knew John would be too.

All the professors mentioned in John's letter and featured in the photos were arrested that day in Judge Sims' courtroom. In addition, Stan Tullock, Mark Vandenberg, Barney Holtz, and Barry Bonds were led away in handcuffs for attempting to flee. Unfortunately, while the bailiffs were apprehending the professors, the two FBI agents, sitting near the exit, left the building in the midst of all the confusion.

"We've had a blowup in the courtroom down in New Orleans," said Rogers, on a cellular telephone call to regional headquarters. "John Walker talked before he was taken care of. Everything's out. The nigger judge ordered all SWAN operatives at the Institute detained for questioning. We need to hide this car while we find out what's known about us."

"You can't bring the car here," said the voice on the telephone. "Take it to the Bennington farm in Ascension Parish. I'll call them and let them know you're are coming."

As Rogers and Beau drove up the long unpaved drive to the farm house, a man came out to meet them. He pointed in the direction of an empty barn. Rogers drove the FBI vehicle into the barn.

"Let's get inside," said the homeowner, after chain locking the barn door.

The three men walked inside the house. There was silence as they waited anxiously for the phone call that would tell them how bad the damage was and what to do next.

"Hello," said the homeowner, as he picked up the telephone. "I see. Right. That's too bad. Okay."

"Let me talk to him!" demanded Rogers. "What's the news?"

"It's pretty bad. We need to get you and Lapiere out of the country. We'll fix the FBI vehicle to make it look like you were in a fatal accident. That way, no more questions will be asked."

"Okay. Get us a plane down here. Let's do it now."

"It's too risky to get a plane out to that farm house. It'll cause too much suspicion with all that's been going on today. We have an automobile with dark tinted windows. We'll leave it for you at the Acadia Hotel. The license plate number is 367-YTN. Lieutenant Carlson will drop it off. Drive the car to Barnett Field in Hinds County, Mississippi. From there, a plane will fly you out of the country."

"Okay," said Rogers. "We're on our way."

The home owner drove the agents to the Acadia Hotel in his Buick LeSabre. They spotted the car with dark tinted windows around back of the hotel. As Rogers and Beau got out of the LeSabre, a tall man with a military bearing got out of the other. He shook Roger's hand and held the driver's side door open for him, as Rogers and Beau got into the car.

The keys were still in the ignition and the car's motor was still running. "Hurry," said Lieutenant Carlson, "they're expecting you at Barnett Field in two hours."

Lieutenant Carlson then got into the LeSabre and he and the homeowner quickly drove off.

As Rogers began to pull out onto the highway, the car exploded. Lieutenant Carlson then retracted the antenna on the remote device that had triggered the explosion. He put the small device in his pocket, as he and the homeowner continued their drive down the highway.

A warrant for the arrest of Rogers and Lapiere for the murder of John Walker had been issued by New Orleans police. The FBI put out an APB for the men.

An hour had passed. Michael and Tisdale were still in the courtroom waiting for the judge's decision. They sat anxiously at the plaintiff's table as Judge Sims reentered the courtroom. As Judge Sims sat down at the bench, Tisdale took Michael's hand and held it. Erroll Fontenot, Dean Frank Hebert, and Henry Murphy were all sitting immediately behind Michael and Tisdale. Carol Sweeney and Edna Auta were still in their original seats.

"I have reached my decision," said the judge, "in the case of *Dr. Michael Woods vs. the Orleans University and the Institute of Public Policy*. Based upon a preponderance of the evidence, I rule in favor of the plaintiff."

Michael smiled widely. Tisdale squeezed his hand. Dean Hebert reached over and patted Michael on his back.

"Evidence presented here this day suggests," said Judge Sims," that it is more likely than not that the plaintiff was indeed subjected to undue racial harassment. It is quite believable, that in such an environment as described here today, that the plaintiff was retaliated against by Orleans University administrators for complaining about what he perceived to be a climate of racial prejudice at its Institute for Public Policy.

"In addition to the rendering of this decision, I must also address other issues which have come to light as a result of this trial. Let it be known that I will recommend to the district attorney that he do a complete investigation into the backgrounds of all Institute for Public Policy professors. This will include those professors who were not present here today as well. The purpose is to uncover any possible collusion with the deaths of Harry Bernstein, Orville Reid and Alex Sanchez. Subsequent to that investigation, it will be determined on what criminal charges the professors are to stand trial, if any. The decision will be in the hands of the district attorney and the grand jury."

Chapter Thirteen

John Walker was dead. No one else alive, with the exception of the Institute professors themselves, had firsthand knowledge of their activities. Facing the possibility of a weak case, the New Orleans District Attorney contacted FBI Director Luis Silverman early the next morning, a Friday, and requested FBI cooperation and a dual investigation.

Realizing the delicate nature of the FBI Report, Director Silverman decided to stick with agents Jeff Kemp and Keith Conlin. They were ordered to fly to New Orleans that Monday and brief the New Orleans Police and District Attorney's office on the FBI report.

"Basically," said Jeff Kemp, in a Tuesday morning briefing, "what the report reveals is that Director Silverman directed a special task force, consisting of me and agent Keith Conlin, to follow the tracks of agents Rogers and Lapiere. This resulted from various but anonymous communication the Director had received speculating that the agents were SWAN operatives."

"How complete is your report?" asked an assistant DA.

"It's not as complete as we'd like it to be. Certain individuals key to the investigation died before they could either finish their work or supply the agency with information. However, although it's not complete, it contains enough information to conclude that Rogers and Lapiere took part in Broussard's death and that they indeed framed and subsequently killed John Walker."

"What's the basis of that?" asked the NOPD chief.

"The report documents evidence," replied Jeff, "that the agents visited the New Orleans area on numerous occasions. Particularly interesting are their unscheduled visits to the area on the dates of Bernstein's death and Tyrone Lockett's disappearance. We speculate that only agents Rogers and Lapiere could have killed John Walker, and this was done in violation of an FBI directive that he be taken alive."

"Michael Woods testified in court that he heard the agents kill John Walker," said the police chief.

"What about the professors at the Institute of Public Policy? What do you have on them?" asked the district attorney.

"Although the agency hasn't targeted the Institute of Public Policy since Broussard's death, phone logs show a highly unusual amount of communication between Lapiere and Rogers and certain professors at the Institute. The agency has no explanation for the contacts unless these professors were indeed a part of the conspiracy as John Walker claimed. The information we have suggests that if Broussard had indeed uncovered a SWAN infiltration of the Institute, such information died with him or was destroyed on its way up the hierarchy."

"We have the photos from the civil trial to fill in that gap," said the police chief. "I don't think any jury will question whether or not they're involved in this SWAN. The problem is can it be shown that they knew about the murders and covered them up?"

"Here we're dealing with guilt beyond a reasonable doubt as opposed to a simple preponderance of the evidence as in the civil trial," said the district attorney. "This will be tougher. We have enough to get an indictment on Lapiere and Rogers but they were killed Thursday, probably by their own people. I don't know if a grand jury will indict the professors."

"I admit that most of the information we have on the professors is circumstantial," said the police chief. "However, I suggest it be given to the grand jury. You never know how they will respond. Meanwhile, perhaps other information will surface."

"As a white district attorney in a majority black city, I don't think I have any choice but to send it to the grand jury," said the district attorney. "And if we don't send it to the grand jury, we could perhaps be sued by the professors for false imprisonment. None of us want that."

The following week the Orleans Parish Grand Jury indicted twelve professors from the Institute for Public Policy, including all nine who had been detained for questioning, and ordered that they be held over for trial. They would be tried as conspirators for the deaths of Harry Bernstein, Orville Reid, Alex Sanchez, and John Walker. Henry Murphy was not indicted.

FBI Director Luis Silverman held a nationally televised news conference later that evening. He did so at the urging of the President of the United States and the Mayor of New Orleans. Michael was at home, lying on his bed and eating a snack, as he watched and listened to Director Silverman.

"Although the agency conducts thorough background checks on its recruits, it cannot completely deny the existence of other extremists within the organization. However, before our special investigation is completed, a thorough internal review will be conducted to rid us of subversives and those who would undermine American ideals and freedoms."

Kathy Walker watched Silverman's news conference from her home. As usual around this time of day, Kathy was in the kitchen. She and Caroline had not fully realized what had happened until they read it in the newspapers and watched the television news reports. Caroline reacted by becoming chronically depressed. She went to her bedroom and did not leave the house for weeks.

With Caroline upstairs in her bedroom, Kathy moved to the den. As she looked around the lonely room, she paused at the sight of the hallway that led to the game room. She slowly got up and walked down the hallway until she reached the room. She flipped on the light switch. There was her husband's collection of shotguns, rifles, and pistols. She leaned against the pool table and stared at the gun case. After about ten minutes, she went upstairs to bed.

The next morning, a Friday, Michael took a nine thirty flight to Chicago. He wanted to spend some time with Jane, and he needed to be away from New Orleans. He called Barbara Tisdale's office early that morning and gave her a telephone and fax number where she could reach him, if need be.

On this same morning, Kathy Walker called the clinic and instructed her secretary to cancel her appointments for the day because she was ill. Kathy had decided that she would attend the arraignment. She wanted to see their faces.

Kathy drove downtown and parked several blocks from the Criminal Courts building. As she got out of her car, Michael's plane was taking off for Chicago. Michael finally relaxed, looking out the window down onto the cars and the people and the small buildings. It reminded him of when he was a little boy back in Tutwiler and the many times he and his mother took the Greyhound bus to Richmond.

Kathy Walker passed by men and women in business suits. They all seemed so happy. A couple of blocks from the courthouse Kathy began to hear the voices of demonstrators. As she got closer, she could see that they were mostly blacks with a few whites thrown in here and there. Kathy gathered that many of them were the more educated and professional blacks because of the way they were dressed. Their voices got louder and louder as they yelled, "No Justice - No Peace! No Justice - No Peace."

As Kathy approached the steps of the courthouse one of her former patients, a young white woman, called out her name from the crowd. "Dr. Walker!" She ran up to Kathy with protest sign in hand. "Dr. Walker. I am so sorry about everything. If there is anything I can do, just let me know."

"Thank you," Kathy responded solemnly.

The woman continued. "Believe me, Dr. Walker. I read about the FBI report in the newspaper; these people will never get out of prison."

"You're right. They won't," said Kathy. She walked slowly ahead.

As Kathy resumed her journey toward the courthouse steps, she heard a loud voice. "Excuse us, ma'am!"

It was a couple of police officers escorting a handcuffed black teenage male down the steps. The officers had apparently confiscated a 9-millimeter semi-automatic pistol from the young man. One of the officers was carrying the gun. There was maximum security at the courthouse.

For a split second, Kathy became apprehensive. She saw a sign: "Only those with official business or close relatives will be admitted inside."

Three armed guards were lined up at the entrance to the courtroom. As she approached the guards, the first one said to her, "Good morning, Dr. Walker, it's very brave of you to show up here today. Are you sure you want to be here?"

"Yes, thank you, officer," answered Kathy.

As Kathy got closer to the courtroom door, she noticed a portable metal detector hanging from the hip of the third officer, who was arguing with a young black man. The young man was upset because the officers refused to allow him into the courtroom. It seemed as if the entire police force had been given a directive to thwart any possible trouble from the city's black community.

As the third officer used the metal detector on the young black man, Kathy slipped into the courtroom.

She took a seat on the last row behind the defense table. The other side of the courtroom was crowded, but the defense side had only two other spectators.

The defendants, all twelve of them, were brought out in handcuffs. Several of them noticed Kathy in the back of the room.

After the procedural matters were taken care of, the judge asked the defendants to all stand. He read to them the crimes they were charged with and asked them to enter their pleas.

"Not guilty."

"Not guilty."

"Not guilty."

"Not guilty."

"Not guilty."

"Not guilty."

Kathy heard "Not guilty" twelve times.

"What a farce," she thought to herself. If money talked, they would all walk. They had the best lawyers money could buy.

After each of the accused conspirators entered a not guilty plea, Kathy could hear the judge speaking to their attorneys, and then to the attorneys for the state. The other two people seated on the defense side had aisle seats. Kathy opened the flap of her shoulder bag and gripped the handle on the modified semi-automatic assault weapon she had taken from John's case that morning. Inside the gun was a 32 round magazine clip.

As she stood up the bag dropped to the floor and all that remained was Kathy and the metal she held. Within a split second she fired towards the front row and mowed down each defendant one by one, not even sparing their attorneys.

The first round hit Mitzie Schultz in the back of her head. As red liquid soaked her short blonde waves, her eyes flickered shut and her body fell limp. As the second round hit Stan Tullock in the small of his back, he jumped forward and stretched out his arms as if he were yelling "hallelujah." Doris Neuhaus turned to look in the direction of the gunfire. As she turned, a round pierced her forehead and blood dripped down between her eyes as they remained wide open.

"Drop the gun, ma'am! Drop it or we will shoot!" yelled the guard at the door entrance, as he pointed a Beretta at Kathy's side. "Drop the gun!" This was the same officer who had used the portable metal detector on the young black man as Kathy slipped into the courtroom undetected.

Kathy dropped the gun to the floor.

"Back away from the gun ma'am!" demanded the officer.

As Kathy backed up, other officers apprehended her from behind. They put her in an arm lock, handcuffed her, and led her out of the courtroom. Kathy's tears ran down her face and her neck.

Ambulances rushed to the courthouse. Demonstrators were held back by a police barricade when they attempted to stampede the building. Officers encircled the entire wing of the structure with yellow crime scene tap. No one was allowed to enter or leave without verification.

"What would you like to drink?" the flight attendant asked Michael, as she passed him a microwaved croissant turkey sandwich and a bag of chips.

"I'll have orange juice and water," said Michael.

Being up in the sky made Michael feel free. He had never felt so tired or so happy. He was looking forward to seeing Jane and spending a week with her at her parent's house.

Back in New Orleans, local television stations showed the courtroom shootings on their noon, evening and late-night news programs. Thanks to this intensive coverage, the black teen who had been arrested for carrying the 9-millimeter semi-automatic pistol to the courthouse was identified by a viewer as being one of the teens who had mugged and killed Orville Reid several months earlier.

The viewer was Mrs. Reid's neighbor. She and her husband had talked to police on the day of Orville's shooting. The young teen, named Roland, already in custody for gun possession, denied any involvement in Orville's death until Mrs. Reid's neighbors picked him out of a police lineup late that afternoon.

"That's him," said the man's wife. "Isn't that him, honey?"

"Yes! That's him," said the husband. "He and another boy were running from Orville's front yard as he lay dying on the ground. We heard the gunshot," the husband said to the police officer. "We looked out of our window and we saw him."

"I didn't shoot nobody," Roland told the officer who questioned him after he had been picked out of the lineup.

"Well, if you didn't, who did?" asked the officer. "The bullet from this gun here matches the one taken from Professor Reid's body."

"Calvin did it!" said Roland. "I just went along with him."

"Who is Calvin?" asked the officer.

"He this dude who live upstairs from me."

"Are you willing to testify to that in court?" asked the officer.

"Yeah," said Roland.

"Why did you do it? Why did this friend of yours do it?"

"It's that Doris Neuhaus. But she told me her name was Nancy. She offered me $200.00 to kill'm and make it look like a mugging. I ain't never killed nobody befoe so I told Calvin. He killed somebody befoe. He told me it was a easy two hundred bucks. Said we could split the money. He said I just had to go along wid him to keep a eye out."

"How did you get to know Doris Neuhaus?" asked the officer.

"I met her in the French Quarter. I needed some money and she gave me some. But I got mad when I heard who she really was and I wanted to kill'er. She was like the SWAN man. You know. It's kinda like she used me to make me look stupid."

"Okay," said the officer, "if what you've told me is true about this Calvin, being that you're a juvenile, I'll see about charging you with a lesser crime. How old is Calvin?"

"He 19. He live in the Florida projects, upstairs from me."

The following day, a Saturday, those sympathetic to the twelve dead professors held their own news conference and questioned how courthouse security could allow an armed woman to slip past their metal detectors. The news conference was the culmination of a day's events highlighted by a protest march led by SWAN sympathizers. They carried signs in support of white rights, white power, and freedom from persecution by a fallen national government. Many of the marchers attended the news conference and displayed their protest signs for the cameras.

"The blood of clean and decent professionals is on the hands of this city and on the hands of this federal government. The people behind me have cried out this day for justice," said the spokesman for the group. "We demand that the United States Attorney General's office appoint an independent counsel to investigate the government conspiracy that resulted in the deaths of these twelve professors who were guilty of nothing but being white and protective of their own cultural heritage."

Dieter Schultz then spoke briefly on behalf of the Pioneer Legal Association. "Beginning this day," he said, "with the power of the PLA, we have launched a concerted effort to hold the government accountable for this atrocity. We demand the U.S. Attorney General's office appoint an independent counsel to investigate these killings. But, regardless of whether it does or not, we have the funds and the ability to uncover the truth. The federal government knows it would be better if they uncovered it than to do nothing and allow us to uncover it."

Michael and Jane had just gotten home from a day of shopping when Jane's mother informed them of the killings. "It's been on the news all day," said Mrs. Redmond, from the den where the television news was on. "This white woman took an automatic assault weapon into the courtroom and killed all of them. I think they say she was the wife of that John Walker."

"How could she get a gun into the courtroom?" asked Jane.

"That's what they're trying to find out," replied Mrs. Redmond.

Michael and Jane sat in front of the television with Mrs. Redmond and watched the news coverage. "Here's the newspaper," said Mrs. Redmond, as she handed the paper to Michael. "It tells you who they were."

Michael, after a week in Chicago with Jane, flew to Tutwiler to spend a month with his mother. It seemed the best place for him to be. How ironic, he thought, that he'd return to Tutwiler, a place he had done his best to escape from to find refuge and safety.

He spent hours in Tutwiler reminiscing about his childhood; like when at seven years old he planted the little magnolia tree that now towered its flowering limbs over the front yard like a protective cover. He thought of when his stepfather Lucius put him and Philip to fighting and how that angered him. He thought of his constant yearning to escape this town along with its backwardness and adolescent cruelty. Yet, now, to his surprise, most of these thoughts were simply fond memories.

It was a Saturday in late October when through a televised news conference, government findings on the New Orleans shootings were made public. Was there government collusion as Dieter Schultz had claimed?

Jane was sitting on the sofa with Michael. The two of them watched. Pearl, who had just entered the room from the kitchen, stood beside the recliner near the window. She gripped the corner of her apron.

"Our conclusion," reported the Independent Counsel, "is that there was no government involvement whatsoever in this tragedy. Kathy Walker acted alone.

"We know that this finding will not sit well with certain fringe elements of the American population. However, the Office of the Attorney General strongly discourages any type of subversive activity in response to this truthful finding. Any individuals and/or organizations deemed to be a threat to the security of this nation will be dealt with swiftly. That is all I have to say. Thank you."

"Well, maybe it's over," said Pearl, as she sat down in the recliner and finally relaxed. Michael got up, leaned over, and hugged his mother. "I think it is over," he said to her.

After talking for a while, the three walked outside to the front yard where they saw Grandma seating herself next to Steve in one of the folding chairs underneath the shade tree.

"I was just telling Steve about that news I just saw on the TV," said Grandma. "They say she was the only one."

"We say it Grandma," said Michael, as he gave her a hug.

Michael then held Jane's hand and felt the diamond ring fitting perfectly around her finger. He admired its reflection in the afternoon sun. "You know," he said. "It really does feel good to be home."

THE END
Copyright

www.ingramcontent.com/pod-product-compliance
Lightning Source LLC
LaVergne TN
LVHW041706060526
838201LV00043B/593